"Alone at last," Clay said quietly. "I have a little unfinished business with you, Jenny. Something I need to know."

"What unfinished business?" she demanded. Seeing the darkening of his gaze and sensing his purpose, she started to step back. But she'd barely moved when suddenly she was in Clay's arms, his mouth covering hers, her body crushed against him. She resisted for no more than an instant before something ignited inside her. Her arms went around his neck and she found herself returning his kiss, her lips as demanding and bruising as his. There was no tender finesse, only fierce hunger. No gentleness, only mindless plundering. There was no giving, just taking, and Jennifer felt herself drowning in waves of sensation.

After long moments, Clay realized how much further things had gone than he'd intended. He had to stop, before it was too late. "Jenny, I've never kissed or been kissed like that. What are you doing to me?"

She was panting, shaking, stunned that a kiss could be like the one she'd just experienced. But she didn't want to let Clay know how shattered she felt. "Why, you've been hanging around cold-blooded city girls too much," she said with a smile. "That little peck wouldn't even hit the lukewarm level on the Silver Rapids Osculation Meter. . . ."

WHAT ARE *LOVESWEPT* ROMANCES?

They are stories of true romance and touching emotion. We believe those two very important ingredients are constants in our highly sensual and very believable stories in the *LOVESWEPT* line. Our goal is to give you, the reader, stories of consistently high quality that may sometimes make you laugh, sometimes make you cry, but are always fresh and creative and contain many delightful surprises within their pages.

Most romance fans read an enormous number of books. Those they truly love, they keep. Others may be traded with friends and soon forgotten. We hope that each *LOVESWEPT* romance will be a treasure—a "keeper." We will always try to publish

LOVE STORIES YOU'LL NEVER FORGET
BY AUTHORS YOU'LL ALWAYS REMEMBER

The Editors

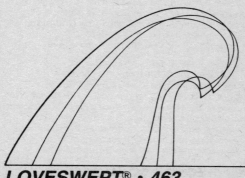

LOVESWEPT® · 463

Gail Douglas
The Best Laid Plans

BANTAM BOOKS
NEW YORK · TORONTO · LONDON · SYDNEY · AUCKLAND

THE BEST LAID PLANS
A Bantam Book / April 1991

TO HANNAH AND HER BROTHERS
For showing us how to stay
"Younger Than Springtime"

ONE

"What do you say I give Parrish a bright red nose?" Jennifer Allan asked with a mischievous smile as she sorted through the contents of the tool box she used as a makeup kit. "A Bozo should have a red nose, don't you think?"

Neil Weston's warm brown eyes twinkled as he laughed and sauntered over to the coffee machine in the tiny television station's green room. "C'mon Jenny, take off your activist's cap," he said as he filled his mug.

"Okay, okay, no clowns," Jennifer said, heaving a theatrical sigh. "How about just a little eyebrow work, then? I'll do some nice pointy ones. Make him look like the devil in—"

"Clay!" Neil interrupted sharply, putting down his coffee to stride toward the doorway with his hand extended. "You're early!"

"Very funny," Jennifer said with a laugh, certain Neil was kidding her. Clay Parrish wasn't due for another ten or fifteen minutes, and even if he had arrived ahead of schedule he'd never have found his own way to the green room.

She looked up, still chuckling. But her laughter died in her throat. Her so-called Bozo was staring straight at her, the expression in his gray eyes quizzical, a bemused smile curving his lips. Jennifer wished the green room were a stage with a trapdoor so she could flip a switch and plummet out of sight.

Though Clay Parrish managed an absent greeting and a firm handshake for the producer he'd met at lunch the day before, he couldn't take his eyes off the embarrassed young woman who'd pegged him as a clown. The truth was, her rich, low voice had added an erratic beat to his pulse. Standing unnoticed in the doorway, he'd stared at her, not sure why she'd knocked the struts out from under him. She wasn't the most beautiful woman he'd ever seen, though she was . . . What? The right word escaped him. *Attractive* wasn't strong enough, *pretty* was totally inadequate, and *lovely* was too soft.

Tall—nearly his height—and willowy, with cat-green eyes and masses of wavy hair in a light golden auburn that seemed backlit by the sun. She looked like a wood nymph conjured up by a midsummer night dreamer's imagination. Yet there was a suggestion of athletic wholesomeness about her.

Clay realized he'd been gaping at her in mute admiration. "I didn't mean to barge in on you," he said at last, though he remained transfixed. "There didn't seem to be any receptionist on duty. Somebody walking by pointed me this way when I mentioned that I was slated for *Showdown*. Should I wait somewhere else?"

Despite her prejudice against Clay Parrish, Jennifer couldn't help thinking how quiet and pleasant his voice was, how unassuming his manner. Dammit, she thought, why couldn't he be a blowhard? Why wasn't he coming on as if he thought he was God's gift to everything and everybody?

Wondering just how early he'd been and how much he'd overheard of her rude conversation, she swore under her breath. There was no excuse for being caught taking potshots at him while she was on the job. She was going to have a chance to get her message across later, when she exchanged her makeup-lady smock for the activist's cap Neil loved kidding her about.

She sent Neil a quick, apologetic glance and was grateful for his teasing little grin. By all rights he should have been staring daggers at her.

Then, as if by some unseen force, she found her gaze drawn back to Parrish's smoky eyes and her pulse began thumping to the beat of a tipsy drummer.

She blinked slowly, trying to figure out what was going on. Jennifer Allan wasn't equipped with the kind of heart that throbbed faster because of an attractive man—and if she were, she would have put in a request for a transplant. She'd reached the age of twenty-seven without showing any signs of her family's hereditary love-addiction, and she wasn't about to start exchanging soulful gazes with some passing stranger at this stage of the game.

After an awkward silence, Neil cleared his

throat, reminding the other two people in the room that he was still around. "Sorry the receptionist wasn't at her desk, Clay," he said with uncharacteristic heartiness as he ushered the visitor over to Jennifer. "And we're glad you're here early. It's a big help. Right, Jenny?"

Busy analyzing what was going on inside her, Jennifer didn't answer.

"Right, Jenny?" Neil repeated, gently elbowing her.

"Right," she said obediently, though she had no idea what she was agreeing to. Another little nudge from Neil jolted her enough to mentally replay his words. She switched on a bright smile. "Right. Yes, of course. It's a bonus to have time to get a guest ready before Harry dashes in and gives me maybe thirty seconds to put on his face."

"You mean Harry Davidson? *Showdown*'s host?" Clay asked, pleased to see Jennifer Allan's engaging smile again, even if it was more professional than personal.

Jennifer nodded, then couldn't resist testing Parrish a little. "That's who I mean, Mr. Parrish. The one and only Harry Davidson, a.k.a. the Grand Inquisitor. I'm told that as a kid Harry asked Santa to leave him thumbscrews and toenail extractors."

The twinkle of challenge in her green eyes caught Clay's interest. The lovely lady was trying to worry him. Foolish girl; she didn't need to try. She did worry him. But not about Harry Davidson. "Grand Inquisitor?" he echoed with an easy grin. "But why would he arrive here in a last-minute panic? I thought the show was taped, not live."

"It is taped. Harry's excitable, that's all." Mildly

surprised by Clay Parrish's unshakable calm, Jennifer wondered if he understood what he was up against. Did he assume a small-town interviewer would be easy to handle? If he did, he was in for a rude shock. Harry was carving out a statewide name for himself in the broadcast business by lacerating his guests.

But as Jennifer tried in vain to break eye contact with Parrish, she began to get the distinct feeling that he could handle the barbs Harry would aim at him. She suspected he could handle anything thrown at him by anybody, including the protest planned by her Silver Rapids Heritage Committee.

She wished to heaven the man would stop staring at her. She could almost see little lightning bolts that were coming out of his eyes and charging her body with a barrage of high-voltage shocks. What she needed was a set of Wonder Woman bracelets to deflect the electricity.

What she needed, she told herself firmly, was to stop being a ninny and start harnessing her professionalism. "Would you care to take a seat, Mr. Parrish?" she asked with quiet dignity, indicating the makeup chair with a vague wave of her hand. Perfect tone, she thought with satisfaction, cool and in control.

Clay nodded and eased himself onto the high, barber-style perch beside the table where Jennifer was working. As she returned to the task of setting out the tubes and jars and brushes she would be needing, it occurred to her that she and Harry's top guest hadn't been introduced properly yet. Wondering if she ought to do the honors herself, she glanced questioningly at Neil, caught his amused expression, and glowered fiercely even though she couldn't blame him for enjoying the situation. The one time in the entire past month she'd been called in on a weekday morning to replace the regular makeup woman, her assignment had to be a man who could rattle her cage and ruffle her feathers.

Neil finally remembered his manners enough to make the introductions. He talked for a few minutes about how much he'd enjoyed chatting on the phone with Maureen Holden, the public relations manager for Parrish and Associates, with whom he'd arranged Clay's *Showdown* appearance.

Neil shot Jennifer a little smile, mumbled something about having to wander down the hall to the studio to talk with the camera crew, and left her to fend for herself. She felt like going after the traitor and dragging him back by the ear. Just because she'd managed to block all Neil's farfetched matchmaking attempts practically since the day she'd met him, he was getting his gleeful revenge by abandoning her to this . . . this stranger who kept *staring* at her, dammit!

Come on, she told herself. Don't let the man know he's getting to you.

But Jennifer was perplexed by the tension she was feeling. Over the years, she'd applied stage and camera makeup to countless attractive men. So why, all of a sudden, should she feel so self-conscious for heaven's sake?

It was that penetrating stare, she decided. It would get to anybody.

Why was Parrish doing this to her?

Jennifer peeked surreptitiously at herself. Were her clothes on backward or inside out? It wouldn't be the first time. She wasn't at her best in the morning, especially after she'd spent half the night engrossed in a spy thriller, blissfully unaware that the station would be making an early emergency call for her services.

But no seams or facings were showing, and her outfit was so normal it was positively preppy—an ivory cable-knit pullover topping a pin-striped tailored shirt and a circular mid-calf skirt in beige cotton.

So what was Clay Parrish's problem?

Jennifer yanked several tissues out of the pop-up box and gave him a tight smile. "Protection," she murmured as she cautiously tucked the tissues inside the circumference of his shirt collar, trying to manage the job without touching his neck. The feat was beyond her, and by the time she'd finished forming the makeshift splatter guard for his creamy yellow shirt, gray suit, and striped silk tie, her hands were shaking from contact with his warm skin.

Searching her mind for a rational explanation for why she was getting silly over a man she'd earmarked as her town's Public Enemy Number One, Jennifer finally decided there was no mystery involved.

The problem was simple, and it wasn't just that Parrish kept studying her as if she were under a microscope. It was his self-assured silence.

Except for professional performers, most males submitted to being made up with a great deal of self-conscious kidding about whether cosmetics could transform them, hide their bald spots, or make their double chins disappear. Jennifer usually laughed and explained that she was merely evening out their skin tones for the camera and adding a little powder so the studio lights wouldn't give them a Day-Glo look.

The whole thing was a bit of a power trip, she'd admitted to herself a long time before. She enjoyed having men place themselves at her mercy, even in such a silly, small way. And she liked being in a position to reassure them when they needed it—or make them edgy when they deserved it.

But Clay Parrish wasn't playing her game. He was running some sort of scam of his own. What Jennifer was getting was a sense of *his* power, a feeling that he was permitting her to perform a very personal service for him.

Maybe the red nose had been a good idea after all.

She tipped some foundation onto a sponge and stepped nearer to Parrish to apply it. Almost painfully aware of his sheer physical presence, she struggled against breathing too deeply; the thought of an exaggerated rise and fall of her breasts as she stood close to him was disconcerting, and his lime-scented aftershave was elusive and woodsy-fresh, but as subliminally seductive as concentrated musk.

She began daubing at his forehead with the sponge, using odd little pecking motions, as if he were too hot to touch. "You . . . you don't need much foundation," she murmured, unable to bear the silence. "You have a . . ." She paused at the sound of her voice and cleared her throat. "A great tan," she finally managed in a rasp. She hadn't been aiming for the sultry effect, but somehow it had happened.

Clay smiled up at her. He couldn't help being

pleased that Jennifer was as shaken as he. His skin still burned where her fingers had brushed his neck, and the positioning of the gentle curves of her body had him trying desperately to distract his primitive impulses by dwelling on his last fishing trip. Unfortunately, he'd been about thirteen at the time, much too long ago to do much good.

He thought he'd better make a stab at normal conversation, especially since she'd presented him with an opening gambit. "So do you," he said at last.

Jennifer cocked her head to one side and smiled blankly. So did she what? What was he talking about?

"You have a great tan too," Clay added when he realized she'd forgotten what she'd said to him.

Surprised, Jennifer laughed. It was a nervous laugh. She hated it when her laugh sounded nervous. And it almost never did. "I don't have a great tan," she protested mildly. "I don't spend much time in the sun."

Clay grinned and relaxed a little. "But a light tan *is* a great one in these days of thinned-out ozone layers and warnings from worried dermatologists."

"Yet you ignore the warnings?" Jennifer said, relieved he was trying to chat with her like a normal person. Now if she could just get him to aim his twin lasers of eyes in a different direction . . . "Mad dogs and Englishmen and Clay Parrish go out in the midday sun?" she added.

"Not really," he answered. "I do play a lot of early morning tennis, but I'm naturally dark thanks to the tempestuous Spaniard who enticed my blond, blue-eyed grandmother away from the upstanding young Philadelphia lawyer her family had picked out for her."

"Sounds like a romantic little tale," Jennifer murmured.

"It is. My family history is riddled with romantic stories, Miss Allan. If you'd be interested in hearing the details, maybe we could have coffee together after the—"

"Shut your eyes, please," she interrupted. The last thing she needed to hear about was another family's romantic history; her own heritage was riddled with broken hearts and wilted flowers.

Clay remained quiet while Jennifer applied a light film of makeup to the area under his brows. He wondered if his antennae had scrambled some messages; he'd have sworn that she was experiencing the same feelings he was. Yet she'd cut off his invitation before he'd finished issuing it.

Probably it was just as well, he told himself. He wasn't in the habit of trying to make time with the local ladies in the towns that hired his services; the idea of being the urban-planner equivalent of a sailor with a girl in every port had never appealed to him. And he'd been extra cautious about women lately. He was amazed that he'd given in to his impulse to try to get to know this particular female. Something about her gave him the strong feeling she wasn't the type for a casual fling, and until he got a few things sorted out he couldn't afford to take a chance on getting involved in anything more.

When she began blending the foundation along the sides of his nose, Clay opened his eyes and watched her again.

Jennifer decided it was time to be blunt. "Why are you doing that, Mr. Parrish?"

He favored her with a look of puzzled innocence. "Doing what, Miss Allan?"

"You're . . . you're invading my space."

"What do you mean? I'm just sitting here obeying your every command," he protested with a barely suppressed smile. He found it impossible not to enjoy the little rushes of excitement she kept arousing in him.

"You know exactly what I mean," Jennifer said evenly. "The normal thing for you to do in this situation is look *through* me, Mr. Parrish. There's a special see-nothing stare that people use when they're being made up—especially men. You're not doing it. You're looking *at* me."

"Am I making you uncomfortable?" Clay asked, no longer trying to hold back his grin.

"A little," was all Jennifer would concede. "Do you always flirt with makeup ladies?"

"I'm not looking *at* you in a conscious effort to flirt, Miss Allan. In fact, I'm trying very hard *not* to flirt with you. But I *can't* look through you. It'd be a criminal waste, like ignoring a spectacular sunset. The man who doesn't enjoy you when he has the chance is an unappreciative fool who deserves to be stripped of his girl-watching privileges."

Jennifer stared in amazement at him for several moments, then burst out laughing. "I wish I'd had a tape recorder running during that little speech. It was worth preserving—though I suspect there's plenty more sweet talk where that came from."

"Never having spouted flowery prose before, I wouldn't know," Clay said with a grin that belied his underlying sincerity. He was as taken aback as

Jennifer by everything he was doing and saying. Maybe more so. Surely she was used to men falling all over her, but he wasn't used to doing it. "Listen, if you're not available to have coffee with me, how about dinner?" he heard himself asking. Another shock. Had the strain of the past year finally gotten to him? "We could explore the potential of my budding eloquence," he added feebly.

"Close your mouth, please," Jennifer said, deciding it was time to work on the area around his disturbingly well sculpted lips. "And stop grinning," she added with a feeble effort at a scowl. "You have dimples. I'll miss the indentations and you'll have funny white marks when you're not smiling."

"As long as you're around, I'll probably keep on smiling," Clay argued, suddenly feeling self-conscious enough to want to turn the tables on the woman. "You have dimples yourself, Jennifer. Real beauties, even when you're trying not to show them, like now. There's one . . ."

Jennifer rolled her eyes as she placed her thumb on the end of his nose, her index finger under his chin, and gently shut his mouth. "Now look up at the ceiling," she ordered.

"Why do I have to keep my mouth closed?" he asked. "You're not doing lip and eye makeup."

"I will if you don't do as I say. And you know perfectly well why I want you to count the ceiling tiles and cut the chatter." She smoothed the foundation over his chiseled jawline, reluctantly noting that he had wonderful bones. Strength was etched in every line and plane of his face, his almost craggy features softened only by his irrepressible grin and devilishly twinkling eyes.

She told herself she should have been prepared for Clay Parrish's physical appeal. After all, she'd seen his picture in the local papers and on television news clips often enough during the last couple of weeks. It hadn't taken much observation to note that he was tall and lean yet athletically built, or that his sandy hair had an unruly cowlick with an endearing tendency to part company with the short, neat cut and drift waywardly over his forehead.

But she hadn't anticipated the sheer charisma of the man. She hadn't expected the velvety caress in his gray eyes or the sparkle of fun in their depths.

She peeked to see if he was doing as she'd asked, keeping his eyes focused upward. He wasn't. His gaze locked on hers and his lips curved in a lopsided, knowing smile. All at once she froze, unable to look away or finish what she was supposed to be doing.

"You're very gentle, Jennifer," he said, his voice soft and husky.

She swallowed hard. "I'm just putting a bit of foundation on you," she said airily. "It's not as though I'm doing a skin graft." Almost through, she told herself. A last dab. . . . But her eagerness to finish the job was her undoing. The sponge slipped out of her fingers and headed straight for one neatly creased, gray trouser leg.

To Jennifer's relief, Parrish caught the missile before it landed, but she was mortified. She'd never had that kind of accident, not even the first time she'd done makeup more than a decade before, back in her high school drama class. "You have quite the reflexes," she said with a grateful smile. "You just saved me a panic trip to the cleaners."

"Not at all," Clay answered, certain now that Jennifer was as galvanized as he was by the power of the attraction between them. "There's a spare suit out in my car. I always travel with one just in case." He grinned. "A man never knows when he's going to be pelted with tomatoes and rotten eggs—or sabotaged by makeup ladies who think he should go back to Detroit and leave small-town America alone."

Jennifer hadn't blushed since the ninth grade, but she was sure her cheeks were turning crimson. So he had overheard her comments. Should she apologize for everything and get it over with?

Before she could speak, Clay uncurled his fingers and held out the sponge. "I seem to have smeared this stuff all over my hand. Have you something . . . ?"

"Of course!" she said as she took the sponge and put it on the table. She reached into her kit for a towelette packet and managed to purse her mouth the right way so the usually stubborn envelope ripped open without too much trouble. Then, holding Clay's hand, she began wiping the foundation off his upturned palm, then from between his fingers. Big mistake, she thought after a few seconds. If applying makeup had seemed like an intimacy, this small act seemed nothing short of licentious—especially considering the images being conjured up in her mind as she traced his long, tapered fingers and felt their relaxed but unmistakable strength.

"All set," she said after she'd done a more thorough than necessary cleanup. As she inadvertently met Clay Parrish's gaze again and saw his wicked grin, she knew he was aware that she'd gone beyond the call of duty.

Dropping his hand as if she'd been caught stealing, she grabbed a makeup brush, dipped it into some loose powder, and cautiously dusted it over his face as he went on staring at her. She breathed an inner sigh of relief when the task was over. Putting down the brush, she picked up a mirror and held it so Parrish could check her work. She'd found that most men needed to reassure themselves that she hadn't tarted them up, though she didn't think Clay Parrish was the type to be concerned.

As she'd expected, he gave his reflection only a cursory glance, then grinned at her. "I'm grateful not to have a Bozo nose, but I have to admit I'm disappointed you didn't give me the devilish eyebrows. They'd go well with the horns some people seem to think I wear."

Jennifer decided she had no choice left. "I'm sorry," she murmured. "I shouldn't have said those things. I wish you hadn't heard me."

"Don't worry about it," Clay said good-naturedly. "You're entitled to your views. All I ask is a fair hearing so I can win you over."

"You sound pretty confident that you can," she remarked, not certain whether they were talking about his involvement in the Silver Rapids redevelopment project or something else entirely.

"I repeat," Clay said, his voice deliberately soft and intimate, "all I ask is a chance."

Jennifer's pulse went absolutely crazy. Her mouth went dry and she had to moisten her lips with her tongue. "I have a feeling," she said huskily, "that you can be as persuasive as the occasior demands. And that you usually get your way."

Clay smiled. "Are you about to warn me that this time will be different?"

Jennifer noticed he hadn't denied anything she'd said. "I'm not as sure of myself as you obviously are, but I can promise you a battle, Mr Parrish." She certainly *wasn't* sure of herself, she thought. "A battle royal, if necessary," she added more for her benefit than for his.

"Then call me Clay," he said, his eyes alight with anticipation. "I make it a rule never to scrap with anyone unless we're on a first-name basis."

"And you like a good scrap, right?"

"So do you, Jennifer."

"Nonsense. I'm a peaceful soul. A neohippie. A New Age flower child. Tie-dyed T-shirts and all."

"Make love, not war?" Clay murmured.

Jennifer sucked in her breath as if she'd taken an elbow to the solar plexus. There was no denying the excitement it triggered in her. She had to put a stop to this nonsense immediately!

"My goodness," she said sweetly. "I almost forgo to take off your bib."

To her annoyance, Clay tipped back his head and laughed, obviously aware that she was trying to take him down a notch or two.

But as she reached out with both hands to tug the tissues out from under his collar, she touched a throbbing pulse spot on his neck. Apparently he emotions weren't the only ones threatening to overheat and burst into flame.

Maybe emotions weren't the problem at all. Maybe some new flu was going around.

"The excitement, as you must have noticed,

Clay said quietly, his hands moving to span Jennifer's slender waist, "is mutual."

Even through her layers of clothing, Jennifer felt the warmth from his palms and fingers spreading through her body. "Uh-uh," she whispered in sudden, languorous confusion, resting her hands on his shoulders. "The excitement is . . . It isn't excitement at all. It's . . . nerves. You're just edgy about facing Harry Davidson."

Clay smiled and gently but firmly pulled her closer. "The worst Harry Davidson can do is ask me a few tough questions, maybe make me come off second best or even look like a fool for a few minutes. The question is, what are you nervous about?"

Jennifer gazed at him for a long moment, slowly shaking her head. "The real question is, why am I standing here like this? I don't do this sort of thing."

"Neither do I," Clay said, knowing she wouldn't believe him even though he was speaking the absolute truth.

"You don't know who I am," she said, trying to inject a note of warning into her voice even as she found herself drawn closer and closer to him by some invisible force she seemed helpless to resist.

"No, I don't. But I can't think of anything I'd like better than to find out."

Jennifer smiled. "You're very smooth. I'll bet you've had a lot of practice."

"Not really," Clay answered quietly. He willed her to give in to the temptation that was obvious in the dark, moist softness of her eyes and the slight parting of her lips. Without saying a word, he urged her to surrender to the strange spell of the moment.

An odd lightheadedness overcame Jennifer, and she found herself wishing Clay would stand up and take her in his arms. The whole thing was crazy. No man had ever made her feel this way. She wasn't *capable* of feeling this way. It wasn't happening.

But his lips were so close, so tantalizing . . . so firm and warm, she thought in the next instant. So delicious as they parted under the light pressure of her mouth. So hot and minty sweet.

She was stunned by what she was doing. Appalled. Completely, utterly horrified.

Especially when she kept right on doing it. . . .

Two

The sound of footsteps in the hallway registered dimly on Jennifer's mind. For a few insane seconds, she didn't care. The kiss was too sweet to be ended by anything or anyone.

The footsteps stopped. "Neil!" Jennifer heard from just down the hall, as if through a thick fog. Harry Davidson's voice, she thought, not particularly concerned. She deepened the instinctive demand of her mouth, swirling the tip of her tongue around the moist inner circle of Clay's lips to satisfy her sudden craving for the taste of him.

"Yo, Harry!" Neil answered from somewhere in the building while Jennifer cupped Clay's head in one hand, her fingers splayed through his silky hair.

"I need to talk to you before the taping," Harry said in his usual clipped tones.

Dizzy with pleasure, Jennifer pressed herself against Clay's hard, muscular body as he bracketed her hips between his thighs and let his arms slide all the way around her waist.

"I'll be with you in a minute, Harry," Neil said calmly. "I'll meet you in the green room. If Jen's finished with Parrish, will you ask him to come to the set?"

All at once Jennifer came to her senses, rearing back and twisting away from Clay, pressing her palms to her burning cheeks and gaping at him. "Good lord," she whispered. "You're the kind of man I used to warn my mother about."

Clay tried to laugh, but the sound was hollow. He felt as if someone had hit him with a velvet blackjack. He was reeling from the impact of the kiss. Jennifer's lips and the tentative exploration of her tongue had shifted his center of gravity. He was stunned. He was hungry for more. He was totally bowled over.

But Jennifer was even worse, he thought as he saw her expression. She seemed . . . stricken. As if she'd just committed the deadliest of all the deadly sins.

Hearing the footsteps in the hallway start up again and realizing he'd better pull himself together, Clay managed a grin. "What's the matter?" he asked, amazed that he sounded almost normal. "Is this the first time you've ever kissed a man in makeup?"

His playful question was like a cold shower. Jennifer was glad he was treating the unbelievable moment lightly. She forced herself to smile and speak with a touch of worldliness. "As a matter of fact, I've clinched with lots of men in makeup," she answered, seeing no reason to explain that she was talking about stage embraces.

As Harry Davidson strode self-importantly into the room, then paused to joke over his shoulder with someone out in the hall, Clay spoke in a low voice to Jennifer. "Let's continue this . . . this discussion . . . later. Will you still be here after the taping?"

She thought about her schedule—and his—for the hours ahead. "I have to leave as soon as I've done Harry's makeup. I'm only filling in, and there's an assistant here to help you take off your foundation when the taping's over." She gave him a deliberately enigmatic smile. "But I think you can count on running into me again before the day is over, Mr. Parrish."

"Parrish," Harry boomed, letting loose with all the cultivated resonance of his deep voice. "Glad you could make it. How do you like our little town?"

As Clay stood to greet the *Showdown* host, Jennifer busied herself reorganizing her cosmetics for Harry, whose booze-mottled complexion and lingering chin bruises—he'd been punched out by an enraged guest after a taping the week before—required much more artistry than Clay's smooth, bronzed skin.

To her surprise, she bristled as she listened to Harry's phony friendliness. She knew he would attack like a striking cobra the instant the interview began, and she couldn't help hoping Clay was too smart to be caught off guard.

Ridiculous, she reminded herself. Wasn't she looking forward to seeing the Executioner slice this imported urban planner to ribbons? Didn't she want the Skewer to make Clay Parrish think twice about recommending drastic changes to downtown Silver Rapids? Didn't she intend to get in a few licks herself before Clay's get-acquainted-with-the-community day was over? It was irrational for her to be glad Clay was tall enough to look his adversary straight in the eye. She had no business being pleased that Clay's low but subtly strong voice made Harry's sound rather like the braying of an ass.

Oh Lord, she thought, why had everything she'd done and thought and felt since Clay Parrish walked through the green-room door been so *deranged*? "Okay, Harry," she said with sudden impatience. "Let's get to work, shall we? I know you're up against it timewise." She'd learned the hard way to play up to Harry's self-importance; telling him she had a tight schedule would only make him slow things down, just to remind her who was boss.

Harry settled himself onto the chair and rolled his eyes at Clay. "The slave driver has spoken. But I don't mind a little bullying from Jenny. It's a rare treat to have her make me look good for my public."

Jennifer flashed Clay a quick smile. Harry's posturing always struck her as embarrassingly affected.

But when Clay grinned back at her, she realized she'd done something stupid. She'd shared a private joke with him. Sharing private jokes with a man like Clay Parrish was consorting with the enemy. And Clay *was* her enemy, on more than one front.

Yet she couldn't help slanting a meaningful glance toward Harry, then raising her eyebrows at Clay.

Easily grasping that she was warning him not to fall for Harry's jovial act, Clay was pleased. He winked at her. "I think I heard Neil mention he wanted to see me on the set," he said quietly, noting that Harry wasn't apologetic in the least for not passing on the message. "Where *is* the set?" he added as he started toward the door.

"Turn to your left, then go left again two doors down the hall," Jennifer answered, wondering what Clay's wink had meant. Was it a reminder that there was something unresolved between them? Was it reassurance that he'd run into Harry's type before and was ready for him? Or was it some kind of unspoken promise?

All at once she was profoundly alarmed by what was happening to her. What in heaven's name had possessed her to *kiss* the man? Was she losing her mind?

Jennifer refused to allow herself to hope she might get a chance to lose her mind again sometime. That kind of thinking was high treason.

Ninety minutes after his arrival at the television studio, Clay eased his large frame behind the wheel of his Buick to head for Town Hall and the press conference and open forum that had been arranged by the mayor's office.

As he drove through the tree-lined streets he'd found so intriguingly old-fashioned the day before when he'd done a private tour, he was soothed again by the peace and quiet, the lack of traffic, the easy pace.

Stopped at a red light near a schoolyard alive with youngsters, he was so caught up in watching them play he didn't respond immediately when the light turned green. It dawned on him a few blocks later that nobody had blared a horn at him because he'd been slow on the uptake. He'd always lived in a city, yet every time he visited a small town he felt the same longing, as if he were homesick for a way of life he'd never known.

He also found himself wondering if the children he'd seen in the schoolyard and elsewhere during his first brief trip to Silver Rapids were as happy and healthy as they seemed—so different from the withdrawn little boy who'd kept him at his wits' end for the past year. For a reputed problem-solver, Clay thought with familiar pangs of guilt and frustration, he certainly wasn't coming up with the right solutions for his most pressing concern.

It occurred to him that the last thing he needed was to muddy the waters of his personal life even more than they already were. He'd inherited the job of raising a deeply troubled child; he couldn't handle an affair right now, serious or otherwise.

Yet thoughts of Jennifer Allan kept returning to plague him. He still felt shaken by her kiss. He was thirty-three years old and an experienced man, but that kiss had rocked him as if it had been his first. Jennifer's mouth had been so sweet, so gently demanding and eager, and the scent of her was as tangy-fresh as rain-washed wintergreen.

Drifting into daydreams about Jennifer's hypnotic eyes, Clay was startled by a shrill ringing. It took him a moment to realize that it was his car phone. "If this is you, Mo, I'm sorry," he said as soon as he picked it up, certain the caller was Maureen Holden. He'd promised to check in with his public relations manager as soon as he'd finished with the *Showdown* taping, but he'd forgotten. He shook his head in amazement. Forgotten! "I just finished the Davidson session," he said, stretching the truth a little.

There was a long silence, then the sound of Maureen's throaty laughter. "I tried catching you at the station," she drawled. "I talked to Neil. He said you finished twenty minutes ago."

"I had to wipe off the goop they put on me," Clay explained feebly.

"Didn't the makeup lady do that for you?" There was a definite note of sly interest in Maureen's tone.

Clay's eyes narrowed as he wondered just what Neil Weston had told her. "The makeup lady had to leave before the session ended," he explained with exaggerated patience. "Some earnest young assistant offered to do the cold-cream number for me, but I said I could manage by myself. I managed beautifully. I got the mess all over my collar. I had to go out to the car for my spare shirt and go back to the men's room to change, so there was no chance for me to call you until this minute. I was just about to pick up the phone when it rang." Telling himself he wasn't fibbing too seriously, he wondered why he was making such a big deal of the situation. It wasn't like him.

Maureen chuckled with unabashed skepticism. "Admit it, Parrish. You forgot."

"You know better than that, Maureen. I never forget anything." Clay protested, then scowled. He wasn't forgetful. He wasn't even slightly absent-minded.

Clay blinked as if to check whether his eyes were playing tricks on him. Had he really just seen a sign emblazoned with the words Silver Rapids

Says Good-bye—Come Back Soon? "Dammit," he muttered as he looked at the road ahead and realized that he was heading into farmland.

"What's wrong?" Maureen asked, sounding thoroughly amused.

"Nothing. I missed a turn, that's all." By several blocks, he added silently as he watched for a side road so he could double back.

"Good heavens, it's worse than I thought," Maureen said, laughing again. "Are you not the same man who cased every inch of that town yesterday, who undoubtedly checked each route you'd have to drive today to make sure you knew how to get from point A to point B without any hassles? By the way, I hear she has gorgeous green eyes."

"You hear too much," Clay said in a low voice, a near growl as he executed a fast turn in a driveway and headed back into town. "What were you and Weston doing, anyway? Indulging in idle gossip, or gathering material to write a soap opera? And since when are you so chummy with him?"

"We're not chummy—well, not exactly. We talked a few times when we were setting up the *Showdown* deal, and Neil's just a friendly kind of guy. All he said was that you seemed rather taken with the pretty green-eyed makeup girl and ought to be forgiven for being absentminded."

"If Neil's so impressed with the lady, why doesn't he go after her himself?" Clay asked as he felt a startling twinge of jealousy.

"That's what I asked," Maureen said, sounding as if she were still surprised at herself for the question. "Neil says she treats him like a brother. Treats every guy like a brother, in fact."

Clay smiled. Jennifer hadn't treated *him* like a

brother. "Blame my absentmindedness on spring fever," he said, deciding to get back to business as quickly as possible. "April in the Michigan countryside can do strange things to the mind of any man who's just weathered a Detroit winter. Now, instead of toying with your fond notion that I've met Miss Right, how about updating me on the Illinois project? How does the public response look to the plan we suggested?"

Maureen quickly proceeded to fill him in on the feedback she'd gathered during the past couple of days concerning the redevelopment assignment. Maureen was a good friend as well as a business partner, and Clay sometimes thought it was odd that he'd never been attracted to her, despite her nice little figure, big brown eyes, lustrous auburn hair, and ready humor. But there had never been any sparks between them, which was just as well considering that they worked together.

"Now tell me," she said, rousing him from his reverie, "how did the taping go? Did Davidson put you through the shredder?"

"Harry's not as tough as he likes to think," Clay answered. He didn't feel like admitting that halfway through the interview he'd begun to wonder if Jennifer was the local Mata Hari whose mission had been to throw him off his stride so he wouldn't be up to meeting Harry Davidson's aggressive verbal thrusts. He wasn't even sure whether the sabotage plan had worked or backfired, because Harry had found himself faced with a guest who couldn't seem to stop grinning like an idiot. Clay only hoped his unrelentingly cheerful responses to Harry's attacks on his intentions, principles, and qualifications hadn't seemed frivolous or superficial. He'd intended to remain cool no matter what Harry said, but he hadn't planned on being downright spaced out.

"Clay, talk to me," Maureen said in a singsong voice. "Where'd you go?"

"I'm right here," he answered hastily, beginning to worry about the way his mind kept wandering off. "At least, I'm here now. These cellular phone connections are so damn temperamental."

"Uh-huh," Maureen commented dryly. "Are you headed in the right direction yet?"

"I'll be at the town hall within five minutes," Clay assured her. "I'll call you as soon as it's over."

Maureen gave an unladylike little snort. "If I don't hear from you, I'll assume you've met up with your green-eyed enchantress again."

"Good-bye, Mo," Clay said firmly. "Roger, ten-four, over and out, I'm hanging up on you now."

"Wait!" Maureen yelled. "I have something important to tell you!"

"Mo, I'm at the town hall. I'm parking the car. Say it fast, whatever it is."

Maureen sighed heavily. "A few minutes ago my spies there faxed me a copy of a blistering editorial from this morning's *Silver Rapids Chronicle*. It seems that the publisher, an old curmudgeon named Sam Crane, is dead set against hiring a Detroit urban planning firm—or maybe against any redevelopment at all, judging by the ranting and raving in this piece. The headline is set in the kind of huge type that's usually reserved for announcing the start of a world war. Ban the Plan, it says. Ban the Plan?"

"We haven't even recommended a plan yet," Clay muttered, shaking his head in consternation as he saw the large crowd gathering outside the white colonnaded building. "I don't suppose all the people I see milling about here are a welcoming committee."

"People? A lot of them? Oh no!" Maureen groaned. "Be grateful if they're not—"

"A lynch mob," Clay supplied when he spied the first picket sign, a simple one using the newspaper headline pasted to a piece of cardboard. "I don't mean to be critical, Mo," he said mildly as he shut off the car's engine and undid his seat belt, "but how did this mindless resistance get so out of hand?"

"Clay, we tried to back you up with the usual press releases, but this character is an alarmist spreading the rumor that we'll recommend gutting the entire downtown to put up high-rises, and creating a highway bypass complete with a strip mall to divert retail business and tourism out that way."

"Where did the guy get that idea?"

"Who knows? But it's up to you to neutralize it."

"And right now's my big chance," Clay said. "All I have to do is come up with the magic words to defuse this situation and persuade these protesters to have an open mind. A piece of cake, Mo. Nothing to it."

"You're renowned for your grace under pressure, aren't you? If ever there was a time to pour it on . . ."

"'Make Love, Not Rubble,'" Clay read aloud on another picket sign. "'Mow Down Motown, But Leave Our Town Alone!' Terrific. One word from me and they'll get out the tar and feathers."

"Well, good luck," Maureen said brightly.

"Let's hope," Clay echoed under his breath. Great, he thought disgustedly. The whole project could depend on how well he'd handled himself with Davidson, and he'd been mooning over a woman throughout the interview.

After promising faithfully to report back to Maureen at the first opportunity, Clay hung up and got out of the car. Slipping off his suit jacket and hooking it over his shoulder, he strolled casually through the picketers toward the town hall's entrance. "Hi there," he said to a stolid matron waving a red and white banner proclaiming. Silver Rapids Is Not a Detroit Bedroom! "Great day, isn't it? Have you ever seen a warmer April than this one? I'm Clay Parrish, by the way. Glad you came out to give us your input on the redevelopment issue." He moved on quickly, leaving the woman gaping at him with a bemused half smile.

Clay stopped to shake hands with an earnest young man of perhaps sixteen or seventeen who was wielding a sign that said Divert Tourists from Our Downtown? Parrish the Thought! "I like that one," Clay said with a grin. "You even spelled my name right. I'm Clay Parrish. And you're . . ."

"Raymond Ackerman," the youth said, looking slightly taken aback and shifting awkwardly from one foot to the other.

Clay nodded. "Well, Raymond Ackerman, I'm honestly glad to see you being such a concerned citizen. If you're in a library sometime during the next few days, how about going to the newspaper section and looking through some back issues of out-of-town papers for references to my firm's redevelopment track record?" He ran through a brief list of town plans he'd worked on recently.

"Check it out. You might be pleasantly surprised."

"I'll do that, Mr. Parrish," the boy said firmly.

Clay grinned and moved on. He was almost at the wide marble steps of the hall when he stopped dead. "Jennifer," he whispered, his heart turning over as he found himself face-to-face with her. "Jenny," he murmured, barely restraining himself from an insane urge to reach out and stroke her cheek with the backs of his fingers.

Jennifer had seen Clay approaching and had time to steel herself against his effect on her senses. She'd almost convinced herself that the wildly erotic moments at the television station had been some kind of weird aberration, but the combined effect of his caressing gray gaze, and the way he spoke her name made short work of that theory. "I told you we'd meet again," she said with a tiny smile.

Clay ached to feel and taste her lips again. His arms were straining to encircle her. "So you did," he answered softly.

A sense of unprecedented vulnerability washed over Jennifer. Even the electric moments at the station hadn't sent the tremors through her that Clay's look was arousing now. Seeing him without his suit jacket wasn't helping her stay cool.

Remembering the picket sign she was carrying, she planted it on the ground in front of her. It wasn't much of a shield, but it was better than nothing.

Forced to acknowledge the sign, Clay looked at the neatly block-printed lettering. "'The Heart of Silver Rapids Doesn't Need a Bypass Operation,'" he read aloud, then emerged from his erotic spell and arched one brow questioningly. "What makes you think I'm going to recommend such drastic surgery for your town? Do you believe everything you read in the local paper?"

"My town doesn't have any so-called ills," she shot back, glad to have an excuse to argue with Clay instead of standing around gazing soulfully at him.

"I did a quick tour yesterday, and there are some definite trouble spots," Clay insisted quietly. "I expect a closer look will turn up even more. There are all sorts of buildings downtown that should've been condemned twenty years ago. But the physical problems of Silver Rapids are beside the point. What I don't understand is what you and all these other people are protesting. I'm here on a contract-signing and fact-finding visit, nothing more at this point."

Thrusting out her chin, Jennifer said, " We're exercising our right to express our feelings on this issue before things go too far. It's true that we don't know what you're likely to recommend, Mr. Parrish, but isn't it better for you to hear from the community *before* you draw up a lot of fancy plans?"

"Good point," he said, then frowned as a round-faced teenaged girl dashed up to Jennifer and asked whether it would be a good idea to start chanting yet.

Jennifer shook her head. "I don't think the chant will be necessary," she said, looking embarrassed.

"Chanting what?" Clay asked when the girl wandered off looking disappointed. 'Parrish Go Home'?"

"Something like that," Jennifer admitted.

Clay's frown deepened, creasing his forehead and tightening his mouth. "Jenny, are you by any chance the organizer of this protest?" he asked, his tone suggesting he already knew what her answer would be.

She raised her chin a little higher. "Yes, I am." At that moment a picketer brandishing a Ban the Plan sign wandered by, and Jennifer frowned. "Well, not all of it. I didn't know old man Crane was going to publish that innuendo-riddled editorial in the *Chronicle*, or that he would manage to arouse a knee-jerk reaction from people who couldn't have cared less about the redevelopment question yesterday, but I did suggest to the Heritage Committee that we come out in full force. As I said, we want you to understand—"

"I know what you said, Jenny," Clay cut in, feeling oddly betrayed. "Why didn't you tell me back at the TV station that you were my chief adversary in this town?"

"Because I was there to do makeup, not to discuss local politics. Besides, I'm not your chief adversary, as you put it. Unlike Crane and some of your other opponents here, I'll listen to your proposals and try to keep an open mind. All I ask is that you listen to the community's concerns the same way." Jennifer paused, then added for no reason she could understand, "And since when do you call me Jenny?"

"It suits you," he said, suddenly grinning. "Would you prefer Jennifer?"

She shook her head and laughed, realizing that she'd started grasping at straws to keep arguing with Clay—anything to dissipate his impact on her. "It doesn't matter. I'll answer to just about anything but Fuzzy-Wuzzy."

"Why would anyone call you Fuzzy-Wuzzy?"

Jennifer wished she hadn't blurted out the nickname that had been the bane of her adolescence. "Have you noticed my hair, Mr. Parrish?" she said, reaching up to splay her fingers through the wild curls, as if the instinctive gesture would finally tame the untamable.

"The name's Clay, remember? And yes, I've noticed your hair." It would be difficult not to notice it, he mused. Even if the masses of long, thick waves hadn't been Jennifer's most dramatic feature, her absentminded habit of tossing her head whenever several locks fell over one eye would draw attention to the halo of spun silk glinting red-gold in the afternoon sun. "It's gorgeous hair," he said almost reverently, then felt a little silly and launched into a spoof of his adolescent awe. "It belongs in the Hair Hall of Fame! It's the most—"

"Stop!" Jennifer said, chuckling, unable to mask her reluctant delight. "Save your eloquence for the crowd." She glanced up toward the building's entrance and saw a small, portly man standing by the door, scratching his bald head and frowning as he surveyed the scene. "The mayor's here. Maybe you'd better go join him. He looks as if he could use an ally."

"Okay, I'll go," Clay said reluctantly. "But when do we get a chance to get together more privately?"

She offered a little shrug. "From what I understand, your schedule is pretty tight for the rest of of the day, and well into the evening. And so's mine."

"We have to see each other," Clay urged, surprising himself. Coaxing a woman wasn't his style.

Jennifer flashed him another of her tiny, mysterious smiles. "Don't worry, Clay," she promised softly. "We'll see each other."

He raised one brow as a thought struck him. "Are you going to picket me wherever I go today?"

She shook her head. "Not unless you stand up in the town hall meeting and announce a scheme to bring in a demolition crew to swing a wreckers' ball on Main Street."

"And if it comes to that? If I find I have to recommend knocking down a few dilapidated buildings? Will you treat me as the enemy?"

Jennifer studied him for a long moment. "A little voice keeps trying to tell me," she said carefully, "that I ought to treat you as my enemy no matter what you suggest doing to Silver Rapids."

"Why? Why would you feel that way before you know anything about me?"

"Because I know what I *need* to know about you," she answered. "You're trouble," she said, then gave a strained laugh. "With a capital T—that rhymes with P, which stands for Parrish."

Before Clay could say a word in self-defense, Jennifer turned and strode away, waving her picket sign like a battle standard on a field of war.

Clay gazed after her for several moments, then took a deep breath and headed for the impatiently waiting Mayor Foley. It was time to stop acting like a moonstruck teenager and start behaving like the professional he prided himself on being.

Three

The chronic squeaking of the steps leading up to the second floor of the former Rogers Department Store was a chorus of wooden protests as several bodies mounted the wide staircase at the same time.

Jennifer had only a couple of paragraphs left to proofread in the spring Arts Council brochure, so she kept working to finish the chore despite the flutters of excitement inside her. She almost wished she hadn't known about Clay Parrish's afternoon itinerary; she'd been on pins and needles waiting for his arrival.

Still seated at her desk facing her office door when the delegation of civic leaders—and Clay—reached her cubbyhole, Jennifer looked up with a distracted smile.

"This lovely young lady," Mayor Foley said with a sweep of his pudgy hand toward Jennifer as he and Clay left the rest of their group in the hall and stepped into her tiny office, "is Jenny Allan. She

keeps our local contingent of temperamental artists in line and force-feeds the rest of us a little
culture."

Accustomed to Foley's well-meaning but tire-
some patronizing, Jennifer smiled graciously and
got up to walk around her desk. but she didn't
extend her hand. Touching Clay Parrish was un-
safe. He ought to have a surgeon general's warning
label pasted to his forehead.

"Jenny, meet Clay Parrish, our new town planner," the mayor said with a politician's smile. "But
I think you two have met, haven't you?"

Clay was thunderstruck. Jenny kept turning up
like a trick of his imagination—or an incarnation
of his conscience, sticking close to him to make
sure he did right by Silver Rapids. "Yes, we've
met," he murmured, reaching out to clasp her
hand in his even though she hadn't offered it.
"Jennifer Cricket, isn't it? Popping up on my
shoulder every little while to keep me honest?
Warning me that my nose will grow if I don't
respect the integrity of your town?"

"That's right," Jennifer said with an irrepressible grin. Clay had disarmed her again, she
thought with amused frustration. For the past
hour she'd been bracing herself against his bedroom eyes, caressing voice, and bold suggestive-
ness, and he'd done an end run around her
resistance with his frankness and gentle humor—
and that melting touch she'd been so determined
to avoid. But she refused to soften. "And you'll be
seeing stars instead of wishing on them, Mr.
Parrish, if you try to turn this town into an
impersonal dormitory for Detroit commuters." She
was exaggerating a bit; at least a three-hour drive

from Detroit, Silver Rapids wasn't really within comfortable commuting distance.

Foley chuckled with sudden edginess. "She's a feisty one, our Jenny. A lady with strong opinions. And she's worried that your plan is going to mean the Arts Council won't have this office space at its disposal anymore."

Clay barely had enough wits about him to make a mental note to suggest to Maureen that George Foley could use some public relations coaching. The redevelopment project was his personal baby, yet he'd been sabotaging it all afternoon with clumsy comments like the ones he'd just made to Jennifer.

Foley's remarks had set him up like a pigeon for the shoot. He certainly didn't want to start arguing with Jennifer about the details of a plan he hadn't formed yet, but he couldn't pretend to be impressed with what he's seen so far of the building she was worried about. "Exactly what does an Arts Council manager do?" he asked, hoping he was sticking to safe ground. "How do you keep the town's temperamental artists in line and the rest of the community swallowing regular dosages of fine arts?"

"Mayor Foley exaggerates," Jennifer answered, tugging on her hand and shooting Clay an impatient glare when he wouldn't release it. But her very best outraged-dignity expression didn't do a bit of good. His fingers simply tightened around hers. "I just make sure the schedules of the various local groups don't conflict," she said, then gave her hand another yank. As if waking up, Clay let go. She almost fell back, saved only by her determination not to make a fool of herself again.

"Jennifer's being too modest," the mayor said, his smile appearing and disappearing constantly, like a nervous tic. "She does a whole lot more than draw up schedules. Why, Jen's not only the driving force behind the summer arts festival and a good part of the winter carnival, she spearheaded the success of our new dinner theater, she set up a cooperative painting and sculpture gallery right in this very building, she . . ." His voice faded as he looked from Clay to Jennifer and back again at Clay. "So . . . er . . . what do you think from what you've seen so far?" he asked at last. "About the building, I mean. The condition of it. Whether it's worth preserving."

At Foley's last comment, Jennifer tossed her head and used both hands to push her hair back from her face, as if to make sure no one missed the dangerous narrowing of her eyes. "Of course this building is worth preserving, George," she said emphatically. "Sure, it's rundown, but if you start razing and replacing every rundown building in Silver Rapids, you'll wipe out the town's history along with whatever affordable rents are still available."

"The town's history?" Clay said with a quizzical smile. He hadn't wanted an argument, but he wasn't about to back down from one either. "This building not only appears to be of very little historical and absolutely no architectural interest, it isn't filled to capacity, so it's wasting taxpayers' money."

"It isn't always vacant," Jennifer protested. "It's used as a storefront headquarters for all sorts of events—elections, the winter carnival, several festivals throughout the year, even food and toy sorting for the Christmas Cheer drive. You just happen to be here on an off day, Mr. Parrish. And if you think I'm going to stand by and meekly watch you obliterate this building for the sake of some spanking new downtown monument to your ego, think again."

Clay was surprised by her blind stubbornness. "Your office must get pretty hot in the summertime," he pointed out patiently. "I don't see any air conditioning units, and the windows aren't big enough or placed strategically enough to allow much breeze to come in. I imagine the cold winter days can be uncomfortable too."

"I don't mind," Jennifer said, her hands going to her hips as she planted her feet apart. "I can always put on an extra sweater and bring in a fan on a sweltering day."

"Why would you be willing to put up with such discomfort?" Clay persisted, resting his hands on his hips and standing with his feet astride in a mirror image of Jennifer's pugnacious stance. "You wouldn't put up with this kind of office if you were working for an insurance company. Is suffering for the arts part of the image?"

George Foley cleared his throat. "Perhaps we should move on, Clay. . . ."

"Image has nothing to do with anything," Jennifer retorted, ignoring the mayor. "Unlike an insurance company, the Arts Council is a nonprofit organization. We're performing a community service; we can't afford to set up fancy offices. And it so happens that the arts are traditionally the tail-end Charlies of city budgets; if some of us aren't willing to make tough compromises and do without a few luxuries to keep things going, the only cultural event we're liable to enjoy is a one-night stand of Wrestlemania!"

"The people who work at town hall are performing a public service too," Clay argued, "but the switchboard operator has a comfortable chair to sit in. I also happened to see the recreation manager's officer earlier this afternoon, and let me assure you, his floor doesn't sag enough to make his desk list like a torpedoed battleship. And I'm sure he doesn't have to scoop chunks of ceiling plaster out of his morning coffee."

Jennifer instinctively glanced back over her shoulders. Clay was right. The scarred desk that had seen better days at the front of a classroom did have a definite lean to it. The floor did sag. The ceiling was crumbling in several spots. And a couple of times, when she'd swiveled in her chair a little too enthusiastically, it had jumped its moorings and dumped her overboard. Why hadn't she complained? Was it because she'd never expected anything better?

"Give some thought to what I'm saying," Clay went on, sensing his advantage and driving home his point. Jennifer was sincere in her convictions, but she was sadly misguided about the value of the Rogers building. And he didn't like the idea that such a nonissue as the question of whether to preserve the place could keep her at odds with him. "Maybe you arts types should consider using your energies to demand your fair share of the community coffers instead of humbly accepting the few bones tossed your way," he said, grinding out each word with an intensity that surprised even him.

"We really ought to be hurrying along," Foley said

hastily, glancing out the door at the other members of the touring party. "Our schedule doesn't allow for this kind of discussion—"

"Arts types!" Jennifer repeated, her attention turning from her desk and the saggy floor back to Clay. "Do I detect a slight sneer in that phrase, Mr. Parrish?"

"Not in the least, Miss Allan. I'm just curious why people connected with the arts seem to accept second-rate treatment from the powers-that-be who decide how the financial goodies are to be allocated."

"It's the starving-artist syndrome," Jennifer said, her tone laced with irony.

Clay glanced pointedly at the mayor, who was shifting his gaze between Clay and Jennifer like a spectator at a tennis-match who'd just realized that the ball was a live grenade and he had a front-row seat.

"We don't accept the short end of the stick," Jenny persisted. "It's all that's available, Mr. Parrish. That's reality. If there's no budget to dip into, there's no budget."

Clay shook his head in frustration at her blindness. "Jenny, I've seen the new Silver Rapids sports complex, and believe me, your town fathers didn't stint on anything there. Meanwhile, you operate from a shack like this and you're so brainwashed you tell yourself it's a heritage building. This pile of rotting wood was junk when it was erected forty years ago!"

"Off we go," Foley said, by this time hopping around like a boxing referee who wanted to stop a match but was a little leery that both fighters would turn and let him have it instead of belting each other. "We have another three blocks to cover before our four-thirty meeting," he added in a strangled squeak.

Clay said nothing more for a moment, glaring at Jennifer as she glared right back. It dimly occurred to him that his outburst was likely to lose Parrish and Associates the Silver Rapids contract before he'd signed on the dotted line, but he didn't care. Only his genuine fondness for small towns and his respect for the traditions they stood for had prompted him to take a look at the job in the first place, and what he'd seen so far had given him no great hankering to take on the political and practical headaches of this particular project. Besides, the sooner he left Silver Rapids, the sooner Jennifer Allan would become merely a wistful memory.

But there was something he wanted to do before he left her office. Something he was determined to do, even though he knew he shouldn't even dream of it. "You go on down to the car, George," he said at last to the mayor. "I'll catch up with you. Give me three minutes."

"But . . . but Clay," Foley sputtered.

"Three minutes, George," Clay said firmly, his gaze locked on Jennifer's. "I want to talk to Jenny privately, all right?"

As the mayor gave in and left Jennifer's office to join the rest of the group, Jennifer was tempted to go with him. Clay's intense, speculative expression was making her very worried.

But she stood her ground, even when he reached back and shut her office door. After all, she told herself, there wasn't much he could do to her in three minutes, was there?

Several seconds passed. Clay didn't move or speak. He was waiting for every last member of the small delegation to noisily descend the staircase.

It was a stand-off. Eyeball to eyeball with Clay, Jennifer refused to blink. But her pulse was utterly out of control, and she was beginning to have trouble breathing.

Finally the staircase stopped groaning, and after another few seconds the building's front door opened and closed with a haunted-house squeal.

Jennifer and Clay were alone.

She waited for him to say something. And waited. Finally she couldn't take the tension any longer. She glanced over his shoulder at the large clock on the wall. "You've got about two minutes, Mr. Parrish. What did you want to see me about?"

"I have a little unfinished business with you, Jenny," he said, his voice suddenly thick. "Something I need to know."

"What unfinished business?" she demanded. "What is it you need to know?" Seeing the darkening of his gaze and belatedly sensing his purpose, she started to step back. But she'd barely moved when suddenly she was in Clay's arms, his mouth covering hers, her body crushed against him. She resisted for no more than an instant before something ignited inside her. Her arms went around his neck as if she had no say in the matter, and she found herself returning his kiss, her lips as demanding and bruising as his. There was no tender finesse about this kiss, only fierce hunger. There was no gentleness, only mindless plundering. There was no giving, just taking. Jennifer was drowning in powerful waves of sensation.

Clay cupped one hand behind her head, his

fingers lacing through her thick hair in an imprisoning grasp, as if to hold her in place for an even deeper, more forceful possession of her mouth. But he surprised her by drawing back slightly and tantalizing her with light kisses and sharp little nips at her lower lip.

His free hand began moving in insistent circles along her spine, pressing her body against his. As he molded her to him, Jennifer felt the hard planes of his chest, the taut muscularity of his torso, the hot rigidity throbbing against her belly. Driven by a primitive need she'd never known or even suspected was part of her, she sought to capture his teasing mouth for another searing fusion. She circled her hips and reveled in Clay's sudden, harsh gasp and the surge of heat against her thighs. She arched her body, instinctively inviting his touch as he smoothed his hand over her until his palm was filled with her high, firm breast.

It was only then that Clay realized how much further things had gone than he'd intended. He wanted to be rid of the layers of cloth under his hand. He wanted to see and feel every inch of Jennifer's body. He had to stop. He had to stop before it was too late. "Jenny," he said raspily, forcing himself to curve his hands around her shoulders and almost violently push her away from him. He stared down at her, his breathing labored and every fiber of his body rebelling against the sudden denial. He realized how rash he'd been to start something he couldn't finish, to play flirtatious games with feelings he should have known were lethal. "I've never kissed or been kissed that way in my life. What are you doing to me?"

The blood was pounding in Jennifer's temples. She was panting, shaking, her whole body on fire. She'd never known a kiss could be like the one she'd just experienced. She bit down on her lower lip. Experienced? *Survived!*

But there was no way she would admit to Clay Parrish how shattered she was. "You've been hanging around cold-blooded city girls too much," she managed to say with what she hoped was a cavalier smile. "Why, that little peck wouldn't even hit the lukewarm level on the Silver Rapids Osculation Meter." Clenching her fists at her sides, she glanced up at the clock. "I hope you found out whatever it was you needed to know, Mr. Parrish. Because if you plan to keep your promise to the mayor, your time is down to forty seconds. It's been interesting meeting you. I do trust you'll understand, however, if I give you a wide berth from now on." She twisted out of his grasp and moved to the small window overlooking the street. Standing with her back to him, she folded her arms protectively across her middle and watched George Foley pacing the sidewalk below.

Clay took a deep, ragged breath and let it out slowly, then spoke as calmly as he could. "I'll tell you what I just found out. I found out that if I have a grain of sense, I'll go back to Detroit and tell my people I was run out of this town. It'd be the simple truth, not because of the public protests—I've dealt with closed minds elsewhere and I can do it here—but because I already have enough problems in my life, and I've just had all the proof I need that if I'm within a hundred miles of you, Jennifer Allan—"

"Thirty seconds," she snapped, refusing to listen

to any more. All she wanted was for Clay Parrish to leave before he could cause any more havoc. If he would just go away, maybe she could pretend he hadn't given her a glimpse of a Jennifer Allan she didn't care to be confronted with. A sensual, emotional Jennifer Allan. A woman ruled by her passions. "Twenty seconds," she said sharply.

Clay started to speak, but changed his mind and simply turned on his heel and left.

Jennifer stayed by the window long enough to see the mayor laugh and point to his watch. Clay had made it down to the waiting car right on time.

George Foley was a weathervane, Clay decided after spending the better part of the afternoon with the mayor. He would twist whichever way the wind was strongest.

The four-thirty meeting Foley had set up was a revelation for Clay. Various developers and building contractors who had their eye on what could be a lucrative project had gathered together to offer their opinions on what should be done about the ramshackle downtown commercial area and its rapid deterioration.

It wasn't long before Clay realized that the publisher of the *Chronicle* hadn't been too far off the mark after all. The representative of Tyson Properties, a Detroit-based developer whose level-and-rebuild approach to urban renewal Clay was familiar with, was adamant that the core of the town was beyond saving and should be knocked down to make room for tracts of oversize houses on undersize properties.

Exactly what Sam Crane had warned about in

he *Chronicle*'s editorial, Clay mused as he listened to the Tyson vision of the future Silver Rapids. Precisely the Detroit-commuter dormitory Jennifer was worried about. Forget the buildings worth preserving. Forget three-hundred-year-old trees. Forget everything but the almighty dollar.

And George Foley was dazzled.

Clay wasn't. He wasn't impressed at all. Even though Silver Rapids wasn't his home, he felt a tug of loyalty to the place—or at least, to the ideal of the kind of community it represented. The planning assignment was becoming less and less desirable as a project to take on, yet Clay felt increasingly driven to follow it through.

There was one stumbling block: Jenny. There would be no way of avoiding her—or of avoiding the fight with her over the Rogers building. Yet no matter how they might battle each other, he was certain an affair between them was almost inevitable. And then what? Where would they go from the heady starting point of romance? Straight to an unhappy ending? Besides, what he'd told her was true: He had enough problems to deal with already, including a little boy who desperately needed all the time, attention, and emotional attachment he had to spare.

Of course, there was always the possibility that Jennifer had meant what she'd said about giving him a wide berth. She'd certainly sounded adamant enough. Almost desperate, he thought. As if she were actually frightened of him—or at least of something. But the prospect of being in Silver Rapids while she avoided him wasn't particularly appealing.

He listened to the arguments raging within and

around him and saw how easily George Foley could be manipulated. He pictured the projected Silver Rapids Supermall—and started to get excited about the very different ideas already taking shape in his own mind for putting the heart back into the community's core.

He didn't manage to settle the inner debate about what would happen with Jenny. But by the end of the meeting Clay knew what he had to do about Silver Rapids.

When Jennifer finished the day's Arts Council duties at six o'clock, she was alone in the Rogers building. Due at a drama club rehearsal at seven and planning to enjoy a leisurely salad and a bowl of chili at the Silver Dollar Diner instead of racing home to grab something on the run, she picked up the phone and punched out her own number. Even though most people knew where to reach her, she always liked to check her answering machine.

When her recorded voice clicked in after the second ring she knew someone had called, so she punched out the two-button playback code. The next voice was so much like hers it was almost eerie: "Jenny, it's Mom, at four-thirty. I'll be at home for a couple of hours, so if you get a chance will you call me?"

It was the only message; Jennifer hung up and dialed the familiar number in West Palm Beach. Something in her mother's tone gave Jennifer the feeling she wasn't going to be too happy with whatever she was about to hear. History, she suspected, was about to repeat itself.

The dreaded words came right after the initial amenities. "Jenny, I thought I'd head north in July and stay until September," Laraine Allan said.

That much was fine, Jennifer thought. That much was wonderful. She adored her mother. Loved seeing her.

But she waited for the other shoe to drop.

"There's someone I want you to meet."

Jennifer closed her eyes. *Someone I want you to meet.* How many times had she heard that phrase over the years? How many upheavals had it signaled?

"This is different, Jenny," her mother said when the silence had lasted a beat too long.

They were all different, Jennifer thought. But she'd stopped arguing years ago. Some women just couldn't stop believing in Prince Charming, no matter how much proof they'd been given that there was no such person. "As long as you're happy, Mom," she said dutifully, adding the appropriate sounds of encouragement as she took down the details about the planned visit even though she felt like screaming in frustrated disappointment. Somehow she'd begun to think her mother had found a new sense of self with the success of her beachfront boutique. The eternally dependent Laraine, who'd sought in vain for the one man she could count on forever, had learned to count on herself. The hopeless, helpless romantic had become a clearheaded realist.

Or so it had seemed.

"Jenny, try not to sound so long-suffering," her mother said after asking Jennifer to check out cottages near Silver Rapids—something suitable for a quiet honeymoon.

"I don't mean to sound that way, Mom," Jennifer said. "I really don't. It's just—" She stopped abruptly. There was no point talking about all the times when some supposedly wonderful, *different* man had breezed through their lives spreading charm and hope, only to leave devastation and disillusionment in his wake. "Mom, I meant what I said," Jennifer murmured with an effort. "As long as you're happy nothing else matters."

"And I meant what I said, Jenny. This is different. Not just the man. *I'm* different. But I won't try to convince you over the phone. You'll see for yourself. Now, how are you doing? How's that summer arts festival shaping up? Are you managing to book any of the performers you were contacting?"

Jennifer answered enthusiastically, glad to avoid the one subject she and her mother had a hard time talking about, the one subject, paradoxically, that she most wanted to talk to her mother about at this particular moment—the insanity that could make an otherwise reasonable, intelligent woman behave as if her emotions or her hormones or both had knocked the sense out of her.

Four

Clay was surprised to see lights on at the community hall when he arrived at eight-thirty. The door was unlocked, so he didn't have to use the key he'd been given after the visit originally planned for earlier in the day had been squeezed out of the itinerary. But he wondered what the foul-up was; according to the mayor's secretary, the place was supposed to be empty from six o'clock on.

There was a small foyer just inside the rectangular structure's entrance, then another door. It was wide open, and Clay heard laughter from inside, then someone speaking in a clear, pleasant voice.

A familiar voice.

Jennifer's voice.

He blinked. Jennifer's voice? This was getting ridiculous. He must be hallucinating. She couldn't be popping up again!

"That was wonderful," she said, sounding exhilarated. "The best yet."

Clay froze. What had he stumbled into?

"Let's do it again," she went on. "Partly because I loved it, and partly to prove that your performance was no fluke."

Clay's treacherous legs refused his command to walk back the way he had come. Instead, with a will of their own, they propelled him forward.

"Start right at the top," Jennifer said with the enthusiasm of a game-show host. "Really do it for me."

Clay couldn't stand it anymore. Holding his breath, he took one step toward the open door and poked his head through it to peer into the dingy hall.

On a stage at the far end, a lanky teenaged boy in a white cowboy hat was grinning at a pretty blond girl in orange shorts and matching top. The girl was talking, asking a question. Just below the stage, another boy sat at the piano. Raymond Ackerman, Clay realized. He wondered if Raymond had done any research yet into the urban planning record of Parrish and Associates.

Clay's glance followed the direction of the blonde's gaze and found what he was looking for. Out in the center of the room stood a familiar tall, lithe figure.

Jennifer.

She made his heart stop every time he saw her.

The classic look she'd sported earlier in the day was gone, replaced by faded jeans, a white T-shirt splashed with a wild kaleidoscope of brilliant colors, and hot pink sneakers with flowered shoelaces. Her tawny mane of curls was twisted into a loose topknot with tendrils escaping every which way.

Clay stared for a long, yearning moment at the enticing nape of her neck. Letting out his breath on a slow count, he very quietly stepped into the hall but stayed just inside the door, glad the lighting was concentrated on the stage area so he could stand unnoticed in the shadows.

"You're doing fine, Sandra," Jennifer said to the girl onstage. "Don't worry about details. Just let yourself *be* Laurey. When Curly sings to you about this fabulous surrey he's conjuring up from his imagination, really think about the verbal picture he's painting so vividly. You can almost see that surrey, and you're getting excited."

"About some buggy?" the blonde said. "I'm trying, but I guess I'm just not getting into it, Jenny. I mean, isn't Laurey awfully materialistic?"

Jennifer laughed. "She could come across that way, but not necessarily. Think about it. Isn't she thrilled because Curly would go to so much trouble to impress her?"

"But a buggy?"

"Hey, that shinny little surrey is the equivalent of today's white stretch limo."

Sandra giggled and nodded. "Okay, I think maybe I've got the idea."

Clay realized that George Foley had only touched the surface when he'd rhymed off some of the ways Jennifer nurtured the arts in Silver Rapids. She was involved on all sorts of levels, it seemed.

From the little he'd seen so far, he admired her directing style and her manner with the teenagers. He liked the way she looked in her outfit. And he loved the way she moved, all loose and easy, yet taut with compressed energy.

Clay felt a knot of desire tightening inside him.

Suddenly he wondered whether he should be lurking about, but he decided there was no reason to feel guilty. He was at the hall for a legitimate reason, and it was only polite to be quiet and stay out of the way while the rehearsal was going on.

Jennifer began taking backward strides. "Do it like the last time, Curly, but bigger. Relax, open up and let that lovely baritone of yours float out to me. I'm going to the far end of the hall and I don't want to miss a single word or note. Try to keep the teasing, flirtatious feeling you put into it last time. It was great." She pointed to the lone musician. "Okay, from the top, Raymond."

Clay wasn't sure what to do now. He didn't want to interrupt the run-through of the song, but Jennifer, without realizing it, was bearing down on him.

He breathed a soft sigh of relief when she stopped with a few feet to spare, still facing the stage.

Her pep talk seemed to have worked, he noticed, his attention drawn to the youngsters by their surprisingly good performances.

Even when the song ended and Jennifer strode forward to summon the whole cast onstage to go through the title number, Clay couldn't bring himself to speak to her. He was too spellbound.

For the next few minutes he watched Jennifer bouncing energetically all over the place. She was so involved with what was happening onstage she seemed blissfully unaware that she was miming the movements and laughing out loud.

Figuring she would stop as she had before, Clay didn't worry this time when she started backing up. "Terrific!" she yelled as song filled the room.

"Give me even more! Make 'em hear you out on the street! Let 'er really rip, gang!"

Clay smiled as the group responded enthusiastically. She was a regular Pied Piper, he mused.

Jennifer was perhaps two feet from him when he realized she wasn't going to stop. "Jenny," he said. "Jenny . . ." But the kids were belting out their song and she didn't hear him. By the time Clay thought of stepping aside so she wouldn't crash into him, it was too late. On the last note of the chorus she raised both hands like a champion boxer and danced right back into his waiting arms.

He didn't get much chance to enjoy having her there. She let out a shriek, went straight up in the air, and seemingly at the same time, whirled to face him. The blood drained from her face as soon as she saw who he was. "What are you doing here?"

"What are *you* doing here?" Clay countered. "I was told the hall would be empty tonight. I didn't have time to look at the place this afternoon, so I got permission to drop by on my own. Your show's looking great, by the way."

"Who told you nobody was using the hall tonight?" Jennifer said, hoping the violent pounding of her heartbeat wasn't visible or audible to anyone but herself.

"Mayor Foley. He said he'd had his secretary check the Arts Council schedule you sent out at the beginning of the month."

Jennifer realized she was half suspecting that Clay Parrish was following her around, which was ridiculous. In the first place, what he'd said about the schedule was true; she'd switched the usual four-thirty drama club rehearsal to accommodate several cast members involved in a special after-school choir practice. In the second place, it was perfectly reasonable for Clay to turn up wherever she did; the buildings where she spent most of her time were two of the very ones he had to check out as part of his preplanning survey. "I gather you didn't drop the project after all," she said. It sounded more like an accusation than an observation.

"No," Clay answered in a low voice, taken back by the guarded expression in Jennifer's eyes. Good Lord, he thought. The woman was afraid of him. Actually afraid. But why? Surely not because he'd kissed her. After all, she'd kissed him first. "I didn't drop the project," he said quietly. "I'd like to tell you why, if you'll agree to listen. How about getting together as soon as your rehearsal is over? You abandoned me to a lonely dinner, so the least you can do is have coffee with me."

Jennifer frowned. His logic was a little bent, but his timing was terrific. She wasn't going to argue with him while a crowd of curious teenagers looked on—especially when some of them had helped her picket him. "Okay, we'll go for coffee," she said after only a brief hesitation. "The rehearsal's over now anyway. Just let me say a few words to the cast before they leave. Meanwhile, you can do your inspection and decide the fate of this hall. Try to be kind, will you? The place isn't Lincoln Center, but it's all we've got."

Clay nodded. "I hope I can prove to you I'm not the landmark-munching ogre you think I am."

Jennifer shot him a dubious look, then strode to the stage and her brood. "Off you go, guys. Super rehearsal." She turned to the pianist and grinned. "Thanks for another fabulous job, Raymond. You're not only talented, you're the soul of patience."

Raymond merely gave a little nod as he let down the piano lid and picked up his musical score, but his cool act didn't mask the pride in his eyes, and he couldn't quite suppress a pleased smile. While Jennifer was busy with several young people who crowded around her to ask questions before they left, Raymond approached Clay. "Mr. Parrish, I did what you suggested. I looked up some newspaper stories and found out that your record isn't anything like what we thought."

Clay grinned. "Thanks, Raymond. I appreciate your fairness. Have you mentioned your findings to your leader?" he asked with a quick glance at Jennifer.

"I started to tell her before the beginning of the rehearsal, but she wanted to go over some cuts she'd made in the score. I'll try again another time. Anyway, Mr. Parrish, I'm looking forward to seeing how you'll square the two sides of the issue. Feelings are pretty strong."

"They usually are," Clay said, stroking his chin thoughtfully. "And call me Clay, will you?"

"Sure thing. See you around." With a friendly wave, Raymond left.

Clay watched Jennifer, wondering if she really hadn't had time to listen to Raymond or simply refused to consider the possibility that the outsider from Detroit might not be her enemy after all.

"Self-esteem," Jennifer said as she sat across from Clay in the quiet booth at the back of the

Silver Dollar Diner. "The point of the drama group isn't producing *Oklahoma!* It's showing these kids what they're capable of. Making them feel good about themselves. Drawing out their creativity. It's enormously rewarding." She reached for her coffee cup and smiled sheepishly, realizing that her nervousness had made her talk nonstop since they'd arrived at the diner. "Stop me before I get on my soapbox. I tend to go on a bit about my work."

"Just what *is* your work?" Clay asked, sincerely puzzled. Was she going to show up no matter where he went in this town? "Jennifer Allan seems to wear a lot of hats," he said with a teasing smile.

She laughed despite her private resolution not to get too friendly with Clay. "George Foley more or less summed up my Arts Council activities this afternoon. But I couldn't live on what I'm paid there. My main career, if I can call it a career, is offering drama classes, the same way musicians give piano lessons and dancers teach ballet. The makeup thing is just a way to earn a bit of extra money and help out at the station when they're stuck. I also do bridal parties and local fashion shows—which is how I supported myself when I first moved to Silver Rapids three years ago, before the Arts Council job opened up and my drama classes started to catch on. But my schedule does keep me hopping around town, so you'll find me turning up all over the place. The proverbial bad penny."

Clay was surprised by what Jennifer had just revealed. "You moved to Silver Rapids three years ago? You're not even a native of this town you're so determined to protect and preserve?"

"I have every right to do what I can to protect and

preserve Silver Rapids," Jennifer shot back, her eyes flashing. She picked up a spoon and began stirring her black coffee. "I'm not living here by accident of birth; I chose this place."

"Do you have to be so touchy?" Clay grumbled. He knew perfectly well why Jennifer jumped at every excuse to bridle at something he said or did; maybe he did the same thing with her. They both took refuge from their intense attraction with whatever defense mechanism was handy. "How did you happen to choose Silver Rapids?" he asked, hoping to settle on a less difficult subject.

Jennifer put down the spoon and took a sip of coffee before answering. "I spent a few months here when I was twelve. It was my favorite of all the places my mother and I lived in, so when I'd had it with city life and the eternal rat race of trying to make it in professional theater, I arbitrarily decided my roots were in Silver Rapids."

Clay wondered if Jennifer realized how much she'd told him about herself in a few casual lines—or how much more she'd made him want to learn. But he had to tread carefully; that much he'd discovered already. "A theater career was your original goal?"

"Superstardom was my original goal," Jennifer answered with a self-deprecating smile. "But I discovered I didn't have the necessary dedication or the requisite thick skin." She looked at her watch, abruptly deciding she'd whiled away enough time with idle chitchat. "I have to be on my way," she said abruptly, although she had no place to go but home and nothing to do but read a new paperback thriller she wasn't all that thrilled with. "You said you wanted to explain to me why you'd signed the planning contract. But you don't have to explain anything to me. What you decide is strictly—"

"My own business," Clay supplied. "I know. And I'm not really explaining. All I want is to tell you I understand your concerns about Silver Rapids and I'll draw up the plan I consider best for the town as a whole, not for a clique with vested interests. Fair enough?"

The man was irresistible, Jennifer thought. When Clay Parrish trained his beautiful gray eyes on her and acted as if her good opinion meant the world to him, she was capable of driving a bulldozer through the entire heart of Michigan if he asked it of her. "And how do you know what's best for this town?" she snapped.

"It's my business to find out," Clay answered tersely, beginning to lose patience. Jennifer wasn't even trying to meet him halfway, so why was he trying so hard to reassure her? Why should he justify himself to some scared female . . . ?

"Are you going to suggest knocking down the buildings you looked at today?" Jennifer asked.

Clay hesitated, knowing what was going to happen when he answered truthfully.

"The Rogers building?" Jennifer persisted. "Does it get the thumbs-down? The community center? Town Hall itself?"

"The first two don't look to me as if they're worth saving," he said at last. "Town Hall is a different problem. It's a beautiful, classic structure that will require some hard thinking."

Jennifer was gratified that Clay appreciated the Town Hall. She recalled her own thoughts about the Rogers building when she'd left it earlier in the evening, but she pushed that memory aside and told herself it was outrageous that some stranger from Detroit had the power to waltz into Silver Rapids and start decreeing which landmarks would be given a stay of execution and which would be leveled. "So the community hall isn't worth saving?" she repeated, her voice trembling as she slid out of the booth and got to her feet. "Tell that to the kids you saw tonight, Mr. Parrish." She grabbed her white nylon windbreaker off the booth's seat and stabbed her arms into the sleeves. "Tell it to the other drama groups I work with. Tell it to the Barbershoppers and Sweet Adelines and the Operetta Society. Tell it to the seniors who hold Friday-night dances in that hall. Tell them how it's not worth saving. Don't tell me. I won't listen." Turning on her heel, she marched away.

Clay sat perfectly still for a moment, amazed by her outburst. What the devil was the matter with the woman? He had a pretty good idea what was the matter with her, and it didn't have much to do with the redevelopment controversy. But she wasn't going to get away with treating him like a cretin. He jumped up, tossed enough money onto the table to cover the tab, and headed for the door Jennifer had just swept through.

"Congratulations!" he yelled as he strode after her. "You dredged up an excuse to run away! You don't like facing the truth or dealing with powerful feelings, so you just up and leave. Never mind being fair. Forget simple good manners. Don't consider the possibility of honest, civil conversation. Not when you can make a dramatic exit!"

Shocked that Clay had followed her, Jennifer ignored him and walked faster, meeting the be-

mused smiles of passersby with a bland expression. She pretended to be completely unaware o
the lunatic chasing along behind her at full holler
but she was grateful that Silver Rapids rolled up
its Main Street sidewalks by nine most nights so
there weren't too many witnesses to the embar
rassing scene.

"You know as well as I do that there are othe
rehearsal spaces in this town," Clay shouted, gain
ing on her. "There are school gyms, church
basements. . . ."

"Terrific," Jennifer said over her shoulder, un
able to remain silent even at the cost of her dignity
"What you don't seem to understand is that the
Board of Education charges an arm and a leg, and
the churches have their basements booked up
with their own activities!"

"Then what do you intend to do?" Clay de
manded as he rapidly closed the distance between
them. He offered a polite nod and a quick smile t
a strolling couple who'd stopped to stare at him
then went back to haranguing Jennifer. "Will you
use that tumbledown community hall until yo
lose a Sweet Adeline in one of the dips in the floor
Will you keep turning a blind eye to the situatio
until the Silver Rapids Male Chorus brings th
walls tumbling down? Doesn't it occur to you tha
there are better ways to solve the problem?"

"Oh, right," Jennifer said, swinging around t
stride backward, too angry to care who was watch
ing. "All we have to do is *demand* better facilitie
and our obedient town council will present us wit
a miniature Carnegie Hall!" She saw that Clay wa
moving in on her, so she pivoted hastily and all bu
broke into a jog as she tore along the street.

Clay didn't waste any more time arguing. He concentrated on catching up with Jennifer, and within moments he was curling his fingers around her arm and yanking her to an abrupt halt. "Forget the damn community hall," he said as Jennifer faced him, her expression mutinous. "It's not the real issue between us. And quit looking as if you're thinking of taking a swing at me. Let's try being straight for a minute, shall we? You're not mad at me over the hall or the Rogers building or anything else to do with this town's renewal project."

Jennifer's eyes widened with outrage. "Oh no?"

"No."

She tried to shake herself loose, but Clay simply held both her arms in a steely grip.

"So what *am* I mad at?" she said sarcastically, then wished she'd kept her mouth shut. Why would she invite that kind of discussion?

"You're not mad at all," he said firmly. "You're scared."

"Of what?" Jennifer said, rolling her eyes and injecting all the derision she could muster into the two words.

"Of me, obviously."

"I'm not scared of you."

"Then why are you running?"

"Because I'm *mad*!"

Clay couldn't help smiling. "You're scared. You're pale, you're shaking, and you can't look me in the eye. What I'd like to know is why a few kisses should throw you into such a panic."

"A *couple* of kisses," Jennifer protested. "Not a few. A *couple*!" Suddenly realizing she'd just admitted the truth, she tried another line of defense.

"You're just as bad. You came right out and said you were floored by . . . by . . ."

"By the fireworks we keep setting off?" Clay put in helpfully. "Yes, I was scared, and I still am. But you're more than scared. You're acting as if I'm one of the hounds of hell."

Jennifer's lips curved in an unbidden grin. "Now who's being dramatic?"

"I thought it might make you like me better. Who knows? I could become your star performer."

Jennifer suspected a double meaning in Clay's words, especially when she saw the quicksilver glimmer of fun in his smoky eyes, but she pretended not to notice. "I saw the way you played the crowd today at Town Hall," she grumbled. "I listened to your disarming little speech. You've got your boyishly sincere act down pat, Clay Parrish. You hadn't said three sentences before everybody had decided that the big urban planner from Detroit is really just a small-towner at heart."

"Because it's true," Clay said with sudden seriousness. "Give me a chance, Jenny. Trust me, and I'll prove to you that it's true. You don't have a lock on caring about Silver Rapids. I'm concerned about it too. Maybe I'm being conceited, but I happen to think this town needs me right now. Your mayor is a nice enough guy for a politician, but he's naïve. He doesn't know what he's getting himself and the town into with some of the people who are cozying up to him. Look, instead of standing here squaring off, why don't I walk you home—"

"I don't need anybody to walk me home," Jennifer interrupted, panicking again. If Clay walked her home, he might kiss her. Worse, she might kiss him. Or ask him in for a nightcap. There was no end to the troubles that could start over a nightcap. "This isn't New York or Detroit," she went on when he undermined her stubborn resolve by looking a little hurt. "I'm perfectly safe on the streets of Silver Rapids."

"Good. But there's no reason why I can't walk you home. We can talk about our problem along the way."

Whether or not she wanted to, Jennifer fell in step beside Clay as he tucked her hand under his arm and gave her very little choice in the matter. "Which problem?" she couldn't help asking.

"Good question. But I think you know which one I mean. It's the way we react to one another. We've got to quit making a public spectacle of ourselves. We can't go around hollering at each other on the street. We can't be falling into each other's arms at every turn. We have to resolve this situation."

"You just won't let up, will you!" Jennifer said with a heavy sigh. "You're a frustrating man, Clay Parrish. But I'll play along for the time being: What do you suggest we do about this so-called situation of ours?"

Clay made a show of thinking the question over. "I'm tempted to suggest we just go ahead and get it out of our systems. Let nature take its course."

Jennifer stopped in her tracks and looked at him as if his brains were still in the blueprint stage.

"But I wouldn't suggest it," Clay added hastily, sliding an arm around her shoulder and prodding her forward. "I wouldn't dream of it. What I think is that we should try to get acquainted. As friends, I mean. Who knows? Maybe under all this sizzling chemistry there are two people who'd hate each other. A cold splash of mutual dislike would settle our libidos down in a hurry." He didn't really buy what he was saying; after only a day he already liked Jennifer Allan. But there was always a slim chance he could find something unappealing about her if he worked at it.

Jennifer thought Clay's suggestion was ridiculous. She seriously doubted that playing let's-be-friends with him would dissipate the terrible desire he'd aroused in her. He was the kind of man who disarmed and charmed a woman out of her wits. If she let down her guard, she might lose not only her head but her heart. "What I'd like to know," she said carefully after several moments of troubled thought, "is just what you mean by getting acquainted."

Clay tipped back his head and laughed, not sure he himself knew the answer to that question. The only thing he did know for certain was that he wanted to find out why Jennifer was so afraid of him.

He already knew why he was afraid of her.

Five

A week after Clay Parrish's one-day visit to Silver Rapids, Jennifer decided he was a thorn in the soft flesh of her psyche. Nothing serious, but a constant irritation she just couldn't put out of her mind.

When he returned to town for a five-day whirlwind round of meetings and inspection tours that left him no time for more than a couple of quick coffees with her, he proceeded to treat her as just a friend. No kisses, no flirting, no intense gazes. She was pleased he'd decided to be sensible. Extremely pleased. She intended to do the same.

Over the second of the two coffee breaks they shared, Jennifer told Clay she'd watched the *Showdown* tape when it had aired. She admitted that he'd been so unassailably calm he'd thrown Harry right off balance, even that he'd almost convinced her he was the right man for the redevelopment job.

"Almost?" he said with a little grin.

"Almost," Jennifer repeated. She felt a pang of guilt when she recalled how Raymond had tried again to tell her earlier in the evening about Clay's urban-planning record—and how she'd found another excuse not to listen. She wondered why; usually she tried to be an open-minded person. The fact that she was attracted to Clay shouldn't make her less fair to him, yet she really didn't want to discover that he was some kind of hero.

The thorn began to fester as Clay's attitude remained stubbornly platonic. Jennifer found herself reliving that first evening, when Clay had insisted on walking her home. Although she tried to forget his good-night kiss, her imagination stubbornly held onto the spellbinding moment. The kiss had been so chaste, so controlled, so devastatingly tender.

But after all, she kept telling herself, a kiss *was* just a kiss.

Clay spent the weekend in Detroit, then came back to town to continue his redevelopment study. Again, he spared precious little time for Jennifer. One lunch, to be precise. As far as she could tell, he wasn't pining for her in the least. His initial burning desire was a thing of the past. It might never have existed at all.

Friends. They'd managed it. They were just friends. How very wonderful, Jennifer thought as she lay alone and chronically sleepless in her bed.

A public forum on the redevelopment question was held at Town Hall on the Monday night of Clay's third five-day week in Silver Rapids. He claimed to welcome presentations from local groups and individuals; all suggestions and concerns, he said at the beginning of the meeting, would be taken into consideration before any plans were drawn up.

Jennifer was there to table two submissions, one on behalf of the Arts Council, the other for the Heritage Committee.

Her appearance for the occasion was deliberately conservative. She'd used hot rollers to coax her wild mane into soft waves, and she'd teamed an ivory silk shirt with the beige skirt she'd worn the first day she'd met Clay, then added taupe pumps, a wide leather belt, and a cluster of gold chains.

She noticed that Clay was dressing for success as well, though in his case he'd toned down the sophisticated urban businessman look in favor of a more down-to-earth tweedy linen blazer, brown slacks, and an open-necked sports shirt.

She got butterflies just looking at him.

When her turn to speak rolled around and she rose to make what she hoped was an eloquent plea for moderation and respect for the community's traditions, a strange rustle went through the crowd.

The gossip about the town planner and the lady who protested too much had made the rounds, Jennifer thought with a flush of annoyance. She'd hoped that the distant attitude she and Clay had assumed toward each other for the past couple of weeks might have canceled out the effects of their early foolishness, but it seemed the local grapevine had been busy, and memories were longer than she'd realized.

Her uncharacteristic nervousness wasn't helping the situation, she realized. Jennifer Allan wasn't known to be shy about speaking her piece in public.

She decided it was all Clay's fault. Did he have to sit there on the dais looking so self-possessed and detached, his arms folded comfortably on the table in front of him, his whole manner making her feel like an anxious supplicant petitioning a despot?

Jennifer faltered.

She cleared her throat, took a deep breath to fill her diaphragm with oxygen, then made her voice ring out over the speculative humming and giggling to blast Clay Parrish right between the eyes.

Enthusiastic applause and several *hear-hears* greeted her impassioned little speech. Jennifer sat down, her head high, refusing to give in to the childish urge to shrink into her chair.

The clapping and approving rumble of voices stopped with odd suddenness as every gaze swung to Clay.

He'd steepled his hands and was tapping his index fingers on his lower lip, his expression pensive as he regarded Jennifer.

All at once he gave an involuntary little jump, as if just realizing where he was. "Thank you, Miss Allan," he said after a moment, then picked up a list from the table and studied it intently. "May we hear now from the president of the Downtown Merchants' Association, please? Miss Miller, I believe?"

Carole Miller was a smooth-haired blonde with a voluptuous figure that blinded most men to her considerable brainpower. Jennifer liked and admired Carole; at the moment, however, she was experiencing a horrifying and utterly incomprehensible urge to deck the president of the Downtown Merchant's Association, whose presentation was getting such rapt attention from the dais.

She also felt like getting up and throwing her chair at Clay Parrish. *Thank you, Miss Allan,* she mimicked silently. Now that he'd made a conquest of her, she was dismissed and he was on to new adventure.

Not that he really had made a conquest of her, she reminded herself as Carole spoke with her usual low-keyed effectiveness. No man could make a trophy of Jennifer Allan.

At the end of the meeting, Jennifer pretended not to notice Clay shouldering purposefully through the crowd toward her. Using a side exit, she made a fast getaway, went straight home, and crawled into bed with a satisfying blood-and-gore mystery. When her phone rang, she let her answering machine take the message. She didn't listen to it until she got up the next morning.

It was Clay. Even his voice sent shivers through her, so she punched the rewind button and erased him as soon as she'd listened to what he had to say. She didn't need his compliments about her presentation. She had no desire to share another awkward lunch hour with him, even if he did sound ever-so-sincere when he said he needed to ask her a favor. He could ask somebody else. Like the president of the Downtown Merchants' Association.

After her shower, Jennifer towel-dried her hair and scrunched it in her fists to give some shape to the naturally unruly curls, put on minimal makeup, then dressed quickly in a plain white T-shirt tucked into a denim miniskirt. The day was warm, so she didn't bother with pantyhose, simply slipping her bare feet into a pair of low-heeled red sandals.

The Arts Council office was her first stop. It was a brisk ten-minute walk from her place; she made it in seven.

Clay was an *obsession*. The instant she opened her eyes each day, her thoughts went straight to him.

Her body actually ached for him. She longed to feel his arms around her, his lips moving over hers.

The streets where she'd walked with him seemed empty and colorless when she strode along the sidewalks without him. Whatever the weather, the whole town took on a gray aspect when Clay went back to Detroit. He was an addiction.

Perhaps Jennifer Allan was doomed after all, she thought miserably. The hot blood that dissolved common sense was bubbling to the surface at last.

The staircase groans that announced someone's approach shook Jennifer out of her worried reverie. Enough moping, she told herself, forcing her attention to the folder she'd pulled from her file cabinet just before her daydreams had claimed her.

Seconds later she felt her body stiffening, bracing itself.

She sat watching the open doorway, somehow knowing. . . .

He completely filled it. Then he stepped into her office and Jennifer felt as if there was no room left for her, no air for her to breathe.

"Most people return messages left on their machines," Clay said curtly.

"I intended to," she fibbed in a small voice, her throat dangerously constricted. Down, girl, she ordered herself. So what if the man was like a sun god warming her skin with his golden glow? So what if he looked more appealing every time she saw him? So what if the pearl-gray windbreaker he was wearing in place of his usual blazer or suit coat showed off his wide shoulders and inviting chest? Jennifer Allan wasn't aroused. Jennifer Allan wasn't arousable.

Grasping at straws, Jennifer studiously looked at her watch, then arched one disapproving brow at her intruder. "It's just nine-thirty, Clay. I did have other chores to take care of, so I'm afraid—"

"Exactly," Clay cut in. "You're afraid."

Jennifer started to get steamed, but for once she kept the lid on. "I'm afraid," she said with careful and patient enunciation, "I hadn't put you at the top of my priority list. Since you're here now, what can I do for you? Your message mentioned some favor."

Clay glared at her. He was tempted to forget his stupid promises, shut the door, and act on one of the uncomplicated impulses Jennifer always aroused in him along with the more complex, unnerving ones. But he knew he wouldn't. Couldn't. Didn't have the right. The depressing and discouraging weekend he'd put in with his nephew had been a stern reminder of where all his emotional energy had to be directed.

Besides, the more he saw of Jennifer's town, the more Clay realized she was going to end up feeling betrayed by him, whether or not her opinion was justified.

He remembered his reason—or his excuse—for coming to see her. "I've had it up to here with fancy presentations and private conferences with community leaders trying to pretend they don't have vested interests."

Clay was talking business, Jennifer mused, but he'd reverted to his unnerving habit of gazing at her too steadily, his dark eyes as caressing as a gentle, knowing hand.

Unable to sit still, she picked up the folder from her desk and rose to return it to the filing cabinet that was shoved against the wall to her right. "And?" she prompted when Clay didn't say anything more.

A vein in Clay's temple had begun throbbing violently. All of a sudden he couldn't think. He'd learned to steel himself against the flamboyant splendor of Jennifer's hair. He'd managed to put up mental shields against the effects of her green eyes and her brilliant smile. He'd even drawn the curtain on his fantasies about her lithe, enticing body.

But he'd never seen her legs before. Long, slightly tanned, bare . . . the denim skirt hugging her slender thighs and taut hips and sweetly rounded bottom . . .

Jennifer pushed the file drawer shut and turned to frown at him. "What are you driving at, Clay?"

"Driving at?" he repeated, his glance sweeping over every alluring inch of her. "I'm going to make love to you," he murmured impulsively.

Jennifer's heart slammed against the wall of her chest. Surely he hadn't. . . . She must have imagined. . . . "Did you just say what I think you said?"

Clay blinked. Nice work, he told himself. One glimpse of the lady's legs and he'd blown his well-behaved act to smithereens. But perhaps he could retrieve the situation with a little bravado. He managed a tentative smile. "What do you think I said?"

Edging back to her desk, Jennifer wondered how to answer. If she told Clay the truth and it turned out that she'd imagined his incredible statement, she'd be making a complete fool of herself. If she told him the truth and she *hadn't* imagined his incredible statement, she just might end up making an even bigger fool of herself.

She lowered herself to her chair and picked up a pencil. Holding it between her thumb and forefinger, she tapped its eraser end on the desk with a reassuringly even beat. Maybe her pulse would get the hint and settle down. "I have no idea what you said," she told Clay. "You mumbled. It sounded like you wanted to borrow a glove. Anyway, you were talking about being sick of meetings."

Clay suppressed a smile and nodded. "Right. Formal presentations. Vested interests." Jennifer's pencil-tapping was bothering him. He moved to her lopsided desk in one stride, perched himself on the higher corner, and reached out to cover her hands with his. "Nervous?" he asked gently.

"Impatient," she shot back, dropping the pencil and snatching her hands away. She folded them on her lap like a scolded schoolgirl.

"Nervous," he insisted.

"Have it your way. I always get nervous when people refuse to get to the point."

"The point," Clay said with a small grin, "is that I'd like to talk informally to some of the people who'll be affected by the redevelopment plan. I thought the member organizations of the Arts Council might be a good place to start. The artists and artisans whose works are in the makeshift gallery in this building, for instance. And the groups that use the community hall. It might be a good idea for me to observe a couple of rehearsals and talk to the performers, directors, set designers. . . . Even that day when I saw you for those few minutes with your teenagers I got a bit of a handle on what's needed in terms of theater facilities."

"What's needed is what we already have," Jennifer said stubbornly. "The community hall."

"How do you expect me to come up with a plan that includes what the arts community wants, if you won't help?" Clay demanded, getting to his feet and turning to rest his palms on her desk, leaning over it until his face was disturbingly close to hers. "You're letting your personal feelings get in the way of doing your job, Jenny."

"I don't have any personal feelings." Realizing too late what a dumb remark that one was, she went on hastily, "Back to the point. What does all this chatting-up-the-common-folk business have to do with me? Who's stopping you? You certainly don't need *my* permission."

"I was hoping you'd help me identify and meet the key movers and shakers of these groups, perhaps even pave the way for me to observe them in action."

"Fine," Jennifer said flatly, telling herself to keep things businesslike if it killed her.

Clay frowned. This was too easy. "Fine? Just like that?"

Jennifer ignored the question. "Do you have one of my schedules?" she asked instead. "It shows who's using what, when."

Slowly straightening up, Clay shook his head

He didn't know why he'd expected an argument from her, but he had. And the truth was, he'd been exhilarated by the prospect. Just being near her got his blood churning like lava on the verge of erupting; if he couldn't satisfy his body's intense demand to make love to her, he could at least release the pressure by doing battle with the woman.

Jennifer wrenched open a desk drawer and pulled out a sheet of paper. "Here. The May lineup," she said without meeting his eyes. "Check it against your own calendar, circle the best times for you to observe and meet with these groups, and I'll see to it that you're expected."

"Thank you," Clay said quietly. "I'll get back to you before the end of the day."

Jennifer nodded, still keeping her gaze averted.

Realizing he had to leave, Clay started toward the door, then stopped. "How about lunch?"

"Can't. I have a meeting." Realizing she sounded curt to the point of rudeness, Jennifer softened her tone a little. "Thanks anyway."

Clay stepped into the hall.

Jennifer started to heave a sigh of relief. She'd gotten through that little encounter by the skin of her teeth.

"Dinner?" Clay said, poking his head through the doorway.

Swallowing hard, Jennifer shook her head. "I promised I'd help paint *Oklahoma!* sets," she said, her voice strained. "There's a shortage of help for the more tedious jobs."

"Oh. Well, perhaps another time. . . ." Clay disappeared into the hall again.

Jennifer buried her face in her hands. She

wasn't sure how much more of Clay Parrish
presence in Silver Rapids she could take. She'
been so confident that she couldn't feel what h
made her feel.

"Does painting sets take much expertise?" h
asked, leaning on the doorjamb.

Abruptly lowering her hands as she silent
cursed herself for letting Clay see the effect he ha
on her, Jennifer shook her head. "Only the abili
to wield a paintbrush. The house kind, not th
artist kind."

"I painted a fence once. Did a pretty fair job to
It only took a quart of turpentine to clean up th
neighbor's cat, and my denims looked kind of nea
all spattered with white. Would I be considere
qualified to help?"

Jennifer stared at him, aghast. Why was h
doing this to her? Why wouldn't he leave he
alone? "You don't want to paint sets. You hav
enough to do."

"I have a free evening. Anyway, painting se
would be all in the line of duty. What better way fe
me to start getting acquainted with the people
just talked to you about?"

"There are only a few adults involved. The kic
do most of the work themselves," Jennifer argue

"By the time any plan of mine is executed ar
the construction completed, those kids will b
young adults. They're the ones who'll be the ma
users of whatever facilities I recommend."

Jennifer tried another tack. "You'll wreck you
clothes."

"I have grubs with me. I never go anywhe
without grubs. What's wrong, Jenny? Are yc

cared to spend too much time with me? Frightned of the sparks we generate?"

"Six o'clock in the community hall basement," he snapped. "Eat first, unless you like pizza."

"I'll be there," Clay answered with a grin. "And I ove pizza."

Jennifer sat very still until she heard the telltale roans of the stairs and the squeal of the building's front door. When she was certain Clay was one, she folded her arms on her desk and lowered er head to rest on them, her eyes closed, her hole body trembling.

Clay had said he was going to make love to her.

And she was afraid he was right.

Jennifer was fuming as she slapped a bright olden haze on the meadow.

Everybody loved Clay.

The adults couldn't get over the fact that the ick town planner would eat pepperoni pizza raight out of the cardboard box and then dirty is hands for the sake of a high-school play.

The shop-class boys in charge of the set-building peration were inundating Clay with questions out urban planning, architecture, and conruction careers in the big city.

And the girls! What a bunch of ninnies, Jennifer ought disgustedly. They had to be coaxed to ggle coyly on stage, yet all of a sudden they were ttering like hysterical loons. They were fluttering ound Clay on the pretext of helping him paint e surrey, as if they were experts. It didn't take six eople to paint a surrey, Jennifer felt like holring.

She suspected that Clay would be able to d
anything he liked to Silver Rapids by the time he'
finished dazzling its denizens with his just-a
regular-guy charm.

What worried her was the fear that he'd be abl
to do anything he wished to one denizen in pa
ticular unless she could find a way to stop meltin
like an ice-cream cone in a heat wave every time h
looked at her.

She didn't understand why his gaze was still s
smoldering tonight. She'd put together the wors
possible outfit—a baggy black T-shirt under a pa
of denim overalls left over from her Chicago high
school days, when she'd been carrying mor
weight on a frame designed to be slender.

The baby fat had been built-in armor, accordin
to her doctor at the time. Boy repellent. Dr. Slad
had been having a torrid affair with her mother, s
he'd been unusually understanding. And he'
known how to get the right reaction from a
almost-plump teenager. "If you hope to play Magg
the Cat or Blanche DuBois someday, you're goin
to have to trim down some, Jenny."

She had shed the armor within weeks.

But she had put on its outer shell tonight. Wh
wasn't it helping?

"How'd you get orange paint on the seat of you
pants?"

Startled, Jennifer whirled around. Her brus
slashed a streak of orange across Clay's gray swea
shirt.

He looked down at her accidental creativit
"Okay, good," he said, nodding and grinning.
like the effect. Sort of the beginning of a rainbow

"I thought you were painting the surrey."

"I was. The job didn't take very long."

"Small wonder," Jennifer muttered.

Clay laughed. Was it possible that Jennifer was jealous? And of a gaggle of teenagers, no less?

He couldn't help hoping it was true.

"I'm sorry about your shirt," she said, wishing she could get a grip on herself. As a rule she was a reasonably gracious person, and rarely clumsy. She ought to be delighted that he'd helped. She should be thrilled that he seemed sincere about getting involved with Silver Rapids at the grass-roots level. Why couldn't she be pleasant to the man?

She managed a grin. "I think the paint will come out if we catch it right away. I'm about ready to leave, and I have a washing machine, so if you'd like to come to my place for a beer or something . . ." She stopped abruptly. What was she saying? What was she *doing*?

"That'd be great," Clay answered before Jennifer could rescind her offer. He knew he shouldn't go anywhere with her, much less to her place and take off his shirt. But he was incapable of turning down her offer. In fact, if he'd known a splash of paint would break down her defenses, he'd have upended an entire can over his head.

Jennifer nodded, still staring in shock at Clay. She felt as if her will had been commandeered by a secret, daring dangerous self she'd been keeping imprisoned deep inside her for a long, long time.

She had to recapture control before it was too late.

Six

"It's been quite a while since that evening you walked me home," Jennifer said when Clay drove straight to her place without asking her for directions. "You have a good memory."

Clay smiled but said nothing. It didn't take much of a memory to recall where Jennifer lived. She was on his mind all the time. He wasn't likely to forget anything connected with her.

As he parked his car in front of the large Victorian house that had been divided into apartments some years before, he was trying to ignore his conscience telling him to drop her off at her door and go back to his hotel for a cold shower. The charade about cleaning up his sweatshirt was a game he felt he shouldn't be playing.

Hadn't it been suggested to him in no uncertain terms that he shouldn't try to carry on an affair with any woman? Hadn't he wholeheartedly agreed? Didn't he still agree? His "martyr complex," as his last important lady friend had called his preoccupation with his nephew's problems, had changed him, and according to one woman at least, he was no fun anymore.

He switched off the car engine and pensively surveyed the converted mansion's well-groomed lawn, sparkling white siding, and geranium-filled windowboxes. *Do it,* he ordered himself silently. *Tell her you just remembered some chore that won't wait.*

On the other hand, he argued, couldn't he just enjoy a cold beer and a chance for quiet conversation with Jennifer? He didn't have to let things get out of control, did he? After all, he really wasn't a hormone-driven teenager; he was an experienced adult. Mature. Self-disciplined.

Right.

Glancing at Jennifer, Clay noticed that she was as deep in thought as he'd been for the past few moments. Was she regretting her invitation? Was she trying to think of some polite way to send him packing? *Give the lady a peck on the cheek and wish her sweet dreams,* his inner voice nagged, beginning to get on his nerves. "Nice place," he commented.

Jennifer started, stared at him, then looked at the house as if checking to see whether she agreed with his opinion. "You said that last time," she finally answered.

Clay managed a grin. "At least I'm consistent."

"Can I assume, then, that my home is safe from your town plan, even if my office isn't?" Jennifer asked, deliberately reminding them both that they were on opposite sides of the fence on at least one important issue.

"Your home seems to be far enough from the

central area to be missed by my Panzer division of bulldozers," Clay answered dryly. He'd given up trying to defend himself against Jennifer's preconceived notions.

He got out of the car and went around to Jennifer's side to hold the door for her. The perfect gentleman, he thought with a generous lacing of irony. If he were really a gentleman, he would make tracks.

He followed her up the front walk and onto the veranda. "Beautiful night," he murmured, looking up at the brilliant stars.

Jennifer gave him a sidelong glance and a grin as she unlocked the door.

Clay chuckled sheepishly. "Okay, but the night was just as beautiful last time."

They went inside and climbed a steep flight of burgundy-carpeted stairs. To distract himself from the enticing sway of Jennifer's hips, Clay ran his hand along the smooth, dark wood of the banister. "Do you ever slide down this thing?" he asked.

Jennifer looked back over her shoulder at him, her eyebrows raised in amused surprise. "I haven't yet. I've never slid down any banister, come to think of it. When I was young enough to do such things, there weren't any around. Mom and I didn't live in banister-type places."

"You ought to try it," Clay said with only a touch of whimsy. He had the impression that Jennifer had missed out on as much of her childhood as he had of his. Perhaps even more. "Everybody should slide down a banister at least once," he added absently, though he'd never done it himself.

"I'll pencil it into my calendar," Jennifer drawled.

She was caught off guard by Clay's lighthearted comments. He was almost ingenuous, even a little shy. She liked him this way. "Here's my place," she said as they reached her door. Dumb remark, she thought. Would she be fitting her key into someone else's lock?

When Jennifer flicked on the light inside her apartment and closed the door behind them, Clay glanced around the living-dining room and nodded appreciatively. "It's even nicer in here," he said. That was witty, he thought. And a great beginning. Why not chat about home decorating? Anything but what was really on his mind—and Jennifer's. "Did the place come furnished, or is this your handiwork?" he went on, wincing at the feebleness of his attempts at small talk.

"I put it all together," Jennifer answered with difficulty, her voice and breathing constricted by the strange tightness that always seemed to squeeze her chest when she was with Clay in a confined space. She hooked the strap of her shoulder bag over an oak coatrack she'd bought at a flea market during a two-month decorating binge just after she'd arrived in Silver Rapids. Turning to smile nervously at Clay, she realized she'd stopped talking halfway through her answer. "But most of the real handiwork was done by local artists and crafts people," she added as an afterthought.

"Really?" Clay said with genuine but exaggerated interest. He took a quick tour around the small room, glancing at a few wood carvings and pottery vases. "There's some pretty good stuff here."

"I think so too," Jennifer answered. "I've been very lucky. Quite a few of the pieces were thank you gifts for volunteer work I did to help the artists set up exhibitions."

Clay nodded and tried to think of a way to get to the real point of this little encounter—whatever the real point turned out to be. But he drew an absolute blank. The apartment seemed warm and he instinctively pushed up his sleeves to his elbows. It didn't help.

An intricately designed, earth-toned rug covering the middle of the polished parquet floor and defining the borders of the living room area caught Clay's attention as a possible conversation piece. "Was this carpet done locally too?" he asked, trying to sound as if he knew something about the craft of weaving.

"The rug, the carvings, the pottery, the watercolors—this town has more than its fair share of talented people," Jennifer said with a sudden burst of enthusiasm, grateful to have a subject she could go on about at some length. She was in shock. What was Clay doing in her apartment? Since when did Jennifer Allan throw down her weapons, lower the drawbridge to her emotions, and invite the enemy into her castle before she was even asked to surrender? "Silver Rapids is like a lot of small communities that way," she went on as she felt a searing flush spread over her skin and knew it wasn't escaping Clay's notice. He was looking at her in that special way of his, with the penetrating gaze that ignited fires all through her. 'It's a sort of mecca for the kind of artist who doesn't thrive in an urban atmosphere. And people who grow up here aren't distracted by all the things there are to do in a city, so they tend to develop their own creativity. At least . . . that's . . . that's my theory." Her last words trailed off as she suddenly ran out of steam.

"Sounds plausible," Clay murmured, unable to take his eyes off her. Even in her drab, shapeless outfit, she was the most exquisite woman he'd ever seen. And the more aimlessly she chattered, the more she revealed her innermost desires. It occurred to him that in their own roundabout way, they *were* getting to the point of why they were alone together in her apartment.

Jennifer heaved a shaky sigh. So much for the possibilities of that promising topic, she thought, her eyes focused hypnotically on the dusting of golden hair on Clay's forearms. Desperate for something more to talk about, she resorted to the blatantly mundane, her voice strained and breathy, her hands uncontrollably fidgety as she smoothed them through her hair, then rubbed the back of her neck. "Even the couch and chairs were reupholstered at a shop here. I bought them sec-ondhand. They were covered in the ugliest flow-ered velvet you've ever seen." Unable to still her hands, she finally shoved them under the bodice of her overalls just above her waist. "The fabric de-signer must have had a hangover," she mumbled. "Or deserved one."

Chuckling, Clay moved to stand behind the couch and slid his palm over the nubby-textured terra-cotta material that had replaced the ugly velvet. "Really nice," he said, quietly cursing his dull wit even as he spoke. Nice this, nice that. Smooth. What a charmer. No wonder Jennifer was so endearingly nervous. She must be asking her-self what kind of inept male she'd gotten tied up with.

YOU GET SIX ROMANCES RISK FREE...
Plus AN EXCLUSIVE TITLE FREE!

Loveswept Romances

AFFIX
RISK FREE
BOOKS
STAMP
HERE.

Kay Hooper's
Larger Than Life

This FREE gift
is yours to keep.

MY "NO RISK" GUARANTEE

There's no obligation to buy and the free gift is mine to keep. I may preview each subsequent shipment for 15 days. If I don't want it, I simply return the books within 15 days and owe nothing. If I keep them, I will pay just $2.25 per book. I save $3.00 off the retail price for the 6 books (plus postage and handling, and sales tax in NY).

YES! Please send my six Loveswept novels **RISK FREE** along with my **FREE GIFT** described inside the heart! **BR9** 41228

NAME_____

ADDRESS_____APT_____

CITY_____

STATE_____ZIP_____

They looked everywhere but at each other. Then their gazes met, and locked, and spoke the truth without the interference of words.

Finally Jennifer shook herself from the spell. "If you want to . . . to take off your sweatshirt, I'll get you another one to wear," she said softly. "One of mine should fit you; I like them big."

She disappeared down the short hall to the bedroom, and Clay stood perfectly still. Getting his shirt cleaned up wasn't important, he kept telling himself. Playing straight with Jennifer was vital. He'd reached the moment of truth.

He kept his shirt on.

While he waited for Jennifer, Clay gave himself another small tour, concentrating on a minigallery of watercolors. By the time she returned with a navy cotton jersey, he was peering closely at his fourth painting without really having seen any of them.

Jennifer wasn't sure whether she was disappointed or grateful that Clay hadn't bared his chest. Her insides were still coiled tightly with anticipation, her heart thrumming with excited dread. She held out the clean shirt. "I'll go put the kettle on for tea while you . . . while you . . . while . . ." All at once her legs refused to budge. "My washing machine is in the kitchen," she said in a small voice.

Clay's insides were surging with a flash flood of need. Even as his mind ordered him to put a stop to what was happening, his body obeyed a more powerful command. While his conscience ordered him to get out of Jennifer's apartment immediately, his hands were grasping the bottom of his shirt, stripping it off, and handing it to her.

She took it. She dropped it.

Then she dropped the clean one as well and simply stood still, her gaze moving slowly, lingeringly over Clay. His arms were even more muscular than she'd realized, she thought as a sensual languor spread through her like warmed, potent cognac. His shoulders were wide and sleek, his chest hard yet inviting to her hands, the flat brown nipples an irresistible temptation to her tongue, the inverted triangle of sun-bleached hair a pillow for her cheek. Emanating warmth and strength on levels far beyond just the physical, Clay was intoxicatingly male. Jennifer wanted to touch him, to breathe him in and taste him. To know him in every way possible. Her emotional fortress had been breached and overrun by forces she had always considered her enemy.

She moved toward him like a sleepwalker. "You must play tennis bare-chested," she said raggedly. Her mouth went dry; she moistened her lips with her tongue and added in a husky whisper, "No tan lines." Reaching out with one hand, she touched her fingertips to the center of his breastbone where the vee-shaped thatch of hair was thickest, then trailed a lightly scratchy line straight down to the point where it disappeared under his waistband.

Every fiber of Clay's body tightened in response to Jennifer's touch. The weakened urgings of his conscience were no match for the instincts of his body. He wanted this woman. He was gripped by an uncanny sense that she belonged to him, and he to her, that making love to her would be just a physical expression of an already existing truth neither of them could deny.

Yet as she began smoothing her palm upward over his rib cage, he closed his left hand over hers and held it against him, crooking the index finger of his other hand under her chin and lifting until his gaze locked with hers. "Jenny, what are we starting here?" he found himself asking.

Jennifer froze, then blinked as if emerging from deep hypnosis. "Dear heaven, what am I doing?" In one quick, jerky motion she snatched her hand away, bent to scoop up the navy jersey, and thrust it at Clay. "I'll clean up your sweatshirt and drop it off at your hotel tomorrow," she said, starting to move away from him, heading toward the door with the desperate intention of opening it and suggesting that he should leave immediately.

Clay was stunned by her reaction, but his reflexes were quick. He tossed the sweatshirt aside and reached for her, wrapping his fingers around her upper arms and turning her, forcing her to face him. Her eyes were suspiciously moist, her body as stiff as if she'd just weathered a physical blow. She looked as if she felt totally humiliated. But why? "Jenny, don't you know how much I want you?" he rasped.

"Please, Clay—"

"Dammit, I was making a last-ditch effort to be fair! Honorable, for Pete's sake!" Clay knew he should have spoken much sooner, but things had happened too fast. "Jenny, I've been telling myself not to get involved with you. It's not just because I'm in Silver Rapids temporarily, or even because I'm not some hit-and-run lover with a girl in every town. It's something more complicated. I have a situation at home—"

"A situation at home?" Jennifer cut in. She felt

as if she'd just been knocked off her perch into a tank of ice water, like a three-balls-for-a-quarter clown at a county fair. Dropping her hand, she stepped back and stared at Clay. "You have this situation at home," she repeated woodenly, then glared at him. "What's her name?"

Clay scowled. His mind was fogged by desire and her question threw him. "What's whose name?"

"The situation at home. Who is she? Your wife? Your live-in? My apologies to the lady, by the way. And to you." Jennifer's voice was brittle and she was trying to back away from Clay as if just realizing he was a dangerous alien. "I didn't realize . . . Of course, you're not wearing a ring . . . not that a ringless finger means all that much, but for some crazy reason I didn't think you were . . ." She swallowed hard, consumed by embarrassment and suppressed anger. "I didn't realize you were involved in a so-called situation at home. Nice euphemism, by the way. Mind you, if I were the lady in question, I'm not sure I'd appreciate being referred to in those particular—"

"Stop it," Clay said, giving her a gentle shake as her obvious hurt threatened to escalate into irrational fury. "Jenny, do you have to be so quick to jump to conclusions about me? Is it something personal, or do you expect the worst from all men?"

Jennifer didn't answer. Clay had hit too close to the truth.

Suddenly he dragged her against him, and a wave of pure delight washed over her. She'd imagined Clay's hard, naked chest countless times, and she'd already touched him, experienced his warmth, felt his muscle and sinew. But she'd had no real idea of the power and heat of the man. Until he decided to release her, she had no hope of escaping the imprisoning encirclement of his arms—yet the way he was holding her made her feel more like a fragile treasure than a captive. And she didn't want to fight Clay; she wanted to rest her head on his shoulder, rub her cheek against him, trail her lips and tongue over his fragrant skin. But she couldn't let herself be ruled by that kind of feminine weakness. Besides, Jennifer Allan as the Other Woman wasn't a role she coveted.

She kept herself stiff with passive resistance. "You and this . . . this *situation* . . . you have an agreement, right?" she finally managed to say with all the sarcasm she could muster. "You've worked out an open relationship, at least on your side. No strings. You live your life, she lives hers, but you—"

"I said stop it!"

Jennifer shut her mouth. After all, she told herself, this humiliating little scene wasn't Clay's fault. She'd invited him home, and on the flimsiest of excuses. She'd proceeded to try to lure him to her bed. He'd confessed his secret at the first opportunity. Almost the first, anyway.

She remained very still. She *wouldn't* give in. Not to Clay, not to herself. She willed him to release her.

But he didn't. He caressed her back and spoke soothingly, his mouth against her ear. "There's nobody else, Jenny. No other woman at all. I'm talking about a different kind of commitment." He hesitated. To tell Jennifer about his responsibilities to his nephew would lead to a long, sad story he didn't want to get into right now. Jennifer would be understanding. Unselfish. Compassionate. But he didn't want her compassion. He wanted her passion. The passion she'd offered so freely. He wanted her love.

Love, he repeated silently when he realized where his thoughts had taken him. Love.

Had things gone that far for him?

For her?

Suddenly, with tender force, he fisted her long, thick hair in his hand and made her look up at him. "Do you believe me?" he asked abruptly, offering no further explanation. "Do you trust me? Are you willing to take your chances with me?"

Jennifer searched his eyes and finally nodded. She had no idea why she accepted his claim that there was no other woman. She just did. The skeptical Jennifer Allan simply believed the man. Incredible. "Yes," she said quietly.

The single word was like a flame touched to a cannon fuse.

Suddenly Clay was taking Jennifer's mouth in a fiercely possessive kiss, and she was responding with savage eagerness. Their tongues delved and probed and dueled. Their hands moved over each other, pushing at clothes, exploring contours, discovering textures.

As his body throbbed almost painfully with his need for her, Clay pushed her coverall straps over her shoulders, then found the buttons at the waist and undid them. He wanted to see her, touch her, learn all her secrets.

The silly, baggy denims she'd worn as a kind of camouflage slid to the floor; she stepped out of them and kicked them aside, her mouth still seeking Clay's lips and tongue. She arched against him as his hands moved under her T-shirt to the base of her spine to press her against him. He wasn't holding back now. Something had dissolved his doubts and unleashed an aggressiveness that struck a deep, responsive chord in her and dissipated the fears that had made her run from him. She couldn't escape now if she wanted to, and she didn't want to. She cooperated eagerly as he rid her of every stitch of clothing. When he stepped back to look at her and touch her with unabashed boldness she shuddered with primitive excitement.

Clay's elation was unbounded as he brushed the backs of his fingers over Jennifer's tawny-rose nipples and watched them swell to eager erectness. She was alive to his every touch; he felt he could do anything he liked with her, and she would exult in her surrender.

Clay didn't speak as he began gliding his palms over Jennifer's arms, her shoulders, her breasts, pausing there to knead the intriguing softness that was so firm and high and proud. Words seemed intrusive and artificial.

Gently squeezing the rich, creamy mounds, he bent his head to take each tip in turn into his mouth, using his lips and tongue and even his teeth to draw the velvety, budlike nipples into full flower.

Jennifer tipped back her head and gasped as Clay's teasing and suckling sent currents of shocking delight sizzling right to the tips of her toes and fingers and ignited an explosive fire between her thighs.

As if sensing the hot pressure in her, Clay blazed kisses upward until he'd recaptured her mouth, his hand moving in the opposite direction to touch the epicenter of her need.

She cried out his name and clutched his shoulders.

Clay caressed and kissed her, his own need set aside as he gave himself unreservedly to the sweet task of pleasuring her. He was awed by her unrestrained sensuality; her responsiveness was beyond his dreams.

Finally, when Jennifer's whole body was trembling and Clay couldn't bear to wait any longer to feel the warm, quivering length of her against and under him, he swept her up in his arms and carried her toward the bedroom.

As he crossed the threshold, he paused. He wanted to suspend the perfect, priceless moment in time and imprint it on his memory.

He smiled as he surveyed the room. Jennifer's oak-frame bed was covered with white linens, from the lace-edged skirt and pillowcases to the crocheted, fringed coverlet. It looked like a puff of cumulous cloud, soft and cool and inviting. He finally spoke. "I always knew making love to you would be a taste of heaven," he said, intending to sound teasing but unable to keep the deep emotion from his voice.

He set her on her feet beside the bed, then plunged his fingers into the rich tangle of her hair and took the longest, deepest, sweetest kiss he'd ever experienced.

Jennifer had never known a kiss could be so gentle, yet so demanding. It started a wild conflagration inside her. It fulfilled all the dreams Clay had triggered in the deepest recesses of her imagination. It stripped her of false pride and lingering ears. With him, she could be totally, unabashedly female. She didn't have to hold back any part of herself. She didn't have to pretend. She didn't have to deny her deepest yearnings.

Clay caressed her back while her hands began exploring him, her splayed fingers raking through his chest hair, circling and tantalizing the hardening nipples. With her lips and tongue, she explored the same territory again while her hands moved down to work open his belt and the fastenings of his jeans.

His take-charge lady, Clay thought, loving what she was doing—and what she *was*. He reached behind her to pull back the coverlet on the bed, lifted her in his arms again, and lowered her to the cool white sheets. Her forest-green eyes were wide as she looked up at him, her lips full and soft and eager. Clay pressed a kiss to her forehead, then straightened up and rid himself of his clothes.

Jennifer watched with undisguised admiration. "You're magnificent," she whispered as Clay returned to her.

He stretched out beside her and gathered her close, claiming her mouth again while running his hands over her back to mold and shape her body to his.

So many textures, Jennifer thought vaguely: the silky pelt against her breasts; the warm satin of his skin under her palm as her hand glissaded over his taut hip and flank; the sinews under the hair-roughed skin of his long legs pressed against her thighs; the slight calluses on the fingers pressing into the soft flesh of her buttocks.

Her senses were filled with Clay, the heady scent of him, the addictive taste of his mouth, the

warmth emanating from him washing over he
like the waves of a tropical sea. She reached dow
between their bodies to touch him, and drew in
sharp, shallow breath at the heat and heavines
that filled her hand.

Clay groaned her name and rolled her onto he
back, and Jennifer wrapped her long legs aroun
his hips to urge him into her. The need for fusio
was a force that drove them both as they took wha
they wanted and needed from each other, and gav
as if their lives depended on giving enough. Cla
slid his hands under Jennifer's hips and lifted he
so his thrusts took him to her very depths. Sh
opened completely to him, tightening her thigh.
arching and twisting frantically as sensatior
she'd never dreamed of catapulted her higher an
higher.

All at once Clay's movements stopped. He looke
down at Jennifer until she met his dark gaze. Sh
knew what was about to happen, and she wa
moved to tears as she realized that he wante
them to share their peak of ecstasy in every wa
possible.

Then, unexpectedly, she found that Clay's imm
nent climax triggered a sudden reaction in her, a
instant and dizzying ascent to her own summi
"Yes," she cried softly. "Oh yes, Clay. Take me wit
you. Now, please, now!"

He tightened his arms around her and carrie
her straight into outer space where the univers
whirled by in a blur of flashing color and ligh
Locked securely in his embrace, Jennifer soare
with a strange kind of freedom, as if the invisib
chains holding her earthbound had been cut.

For a few perfect moments, she was blissfu

otally at peace. She knew she'd been transformed revocably by this single act, but she regretted othing. Clay's essence was surging into her and he was clinging unashamedly to him. Her separate self had ceased to exist. She didn't miss it any nore than a butterfly missed the confines of its ocoon.

Seven

Much too soon, Jennifer's old fears began settling back into her consciousness, intensified by the unprecedented vulnerability she'd so willingly succumbed to. She realized that she'd surrendered her emotional independence without a thought for how she would function without it.

Clay felt the tension returning to Jennifer's body and wasn't surprised by it. He was shaken up himself. "Scary, huh?" he murmured with conscious understatement.

Taken aback by his honest but unexpected comment, Jennifer tried to laugh, but only a wisp of a sound came out.

Clay began stroking her arm. "We have to do some serious talking, Jenny," he said quietly.

Jennifer stiffened. "Talking?"

"Talking," Clay repeated. "The kind of talking we should have done some time ago, before we made the kind of commitment we just went ahead and made on the basis of sheer faith."

"Conversation is highly overrated," Jennifer said
with another ragged attempt at a laugh as she
shifted her position a little, turning just enough so
she was facing slightly away from Clay instead of
snuggling into his warmth. "And I don't recall
anybody making any commitments."

Clay rolled on his side, wrapped his arm around
Jennifer, and tucked her against him spoon-style.
"Don't try to kid either of us," he murmured.
"Ducking the truth isn't worthy of you. You're
scared, and so you should be. I'm kind of rattled
myself. But we'll both get over it. And now we go on
from here."

Jennifer didn't argue. Clay was right on three
counts: She was ducking the truth. Something
life-altering had just happened. And she was
scared.

She closed her eyes as Clay lightly caressed her
breasts and pressed gentle kisses to her shoulder,
though she thought the wiser course would be to
skitter away and off the bed, cover her profound
nudity, and send Clay packing before he undermined what little control of her destiny she still felt
she had.

The trouble was, the warmth of his breath on
her skin was sending ripples of pleasure through
her, and she felt strangely right in his arms. Safe.
Contented. Home.

"Can you tell me why you're so frightened?" he
asked, gently turning her onto her back and gazing down at her with a tenderness he hadn't
known he could feel.

Jennifer shook her head. "I'm not sure myself.
It's all tied up with certain . . . aspects . . . of
the way I grew up, I guess. But it's . . ." She

sighed heavily. "I don't know. Must we talk right now? Can't it wait? Can't we just be happy for a while?"

Clay didn't answer for several moments. He smoothed her hair back from her face and kissed her eyelids. "Do you have a very heavy day tomorrow?" he asked gently.

"Not as heavy as most," she answered in a husky whisper. "Why?"

Clay smiled and affectionately rubbed his nose against hers. "Because you're going to have a busy night, sweetheart. Remember the rehearsal when your *Oklahoma!* kids performed well and you got them to do it again to prove that the first time was no fluke?"

A tiny smile tugged at the corners of Jennifer's mouth as she nodded.

"By morning," Clay said, lowering his head to the still swollen tip of her breast, "I plan to have proven to you that our first time wasn't a fluke either. And then, sweetheart, we are going to talk."

Exhaustion claimed them shortly before dawn and they fell into a deep sleep, entangled in each other's arms, until the persistent summons of Jennifer's bedside phone roused them from their contented dreams.

"Jenny, did I wake you?" her mother asked when Jennifer's groping finally brought the receiver to her ear.

"No, I'm awake," Jennifer said through a telltale yawn.

"I'm sorry, dear. I never dreamed you'd be sleeping. It's after nine, and you're usually up and around by eight at the latest."

Jennifer rubbed her eyes, trying to sort out the jumble of her thoughts. The sudden awareness of Clay's large, warm body stirring beside her made her sit bolt upright. "After nine? Did you say it's after nine?"

"Nine-fifteen. Are you late for something?"

Jennifer shook her head, then mumbled a reassurance when she realized her mother couldn't see her—which, under the circumstances, was probably just as well, she thought wryly, although a mild cheer would be a more likely reaction than disapproval from that quarter. Laraine Allan had wondered aloud more than once how she'd managed to raise a terminally prudish daughter. Jennifer hadn't had the heart to say she wasn't prudish, just self-protective.

Glancing at Clay, she mused that she'd mislaid those self-protective instincts at some point during the past few hours—or weeks—and she automatically drew the sheet up over her breasts.

Clay reached out and calmly tugged the sheet away in a silent reminder that modesty between them was a thing of the past, then got out of bed and started pulling on his clothes.

Jennifer knew he had to hurry back to his hotel to shower and change in time for a ten o'clock meeting. She was luckier; her whole morning was free. "Is anything wrong, Mom?" she asked, lying back on her pillow.

"Nothing's wrong, really. But something's been bothering me, and I decided to call when I had the gumption to speak up."

Jennifer frowned and raised one hand to push

her thick hair back from her face. "What is it, Mom?" She realized she must sound concerned. Clay stopped in his tracks and stood watching her, his brows raised in a worried question.

"Only this, Jenny," her mother said with a firmness her gentle voice rarely revealed. "When I asked you to scout out a honeymoon cottage, you went ahead and found one, and I'm delighted with the way it looks in the brochures you sent. But dear, a honeymoon is usually preceded by a wedding. I've talked to you several times in the past few weeks, and not once have you asked about it. Not once, Jennifer. Are you so against this marriage you're hoping you can ignore it out of existence?"

Jennifer's jaw dropped and she felt a scarlet flush spreading over her chest, throat, and face. She couldn't believe what her mother was saying, yet she knew it was true. Not only hadn't she asked about the wedding, she hadn't *thought* about it! Was she that self-centered, that befuddled by her feelings for Clay, that wrapped up in her own life?

Or, Jennifer wondered, was her mother right? Did she have a mental block about the marriage? If so, she must not admit it. She had no right to spoil things. "I guess I just thought you and . . ." She hesitated, not too eager for Clay to overhear what she was saying.

"Martin," Laraine supplied.

"I know his name, Mom," Jennifer said quickly. "I'm still a little foggy, that's all. I had a . . . a late night. Anyway, I started to say that I figured you and Martin would simply tie the knot right there in West Palm Beach and come up here afterward. I'm sorry I didn't ask, though. I guess I've been a bit . . . well, distracted." She rolled her eyes and stuck out her tongue as Clay shot her a grin of pure male smugness. "Was I wrong?" she asked her mother.

"Not necessarily, but I'd prefer to have the ceremony in Silver Rapids, with my daughter as my maid of honor. Would I be asking too much, honey? I'm well aware of what I've put you through over the years. You were always there for me, even when you'd begged me not to leap into a situation in the first place. Would standing up for me this time make you feel more like an accomplice than an attendant?"

Suddenly uncomfortable—her mother had a disconcerting habit of hitting the nail right on the head—Jennifer slanted a peek at Clay. He was frowning, obviously puzzled by what he was hearing of the conversation. She didn't blame him.

"Jenny, aren't you going to answer me?" Laraine asked. "Is everything all right there? You seem a little discombobulated."

Jennifer rubbed her eyes with her thumb and forefinger. A little discombobulated? She was in shock. What was Jennifer Allan doing with a virile, demanding, unnervingly sexy man standing nearly naked in her bedroom? "Everything's fine," she lied brightly. "And of course I'd be happy to be your maid of honor. I'm sorry I gave you the idea I was negative about the whole thing. I'm not. Really, I'm not. How could I be? I haven't even met Martin, but he sounds wonderful. And you've known him for a while, haven't you?"

"For two years, as a matter of fact," her mother answered. "We started out as friends. The rest just sort of crept up on us."

Friends, Jennifer repeated silently, glad for her

mother but troubled for herself. She'd always believed that lovers should start out as friends.

Were she and Clay friends?

He wanted to talk, she remembered. Friends talked. So did lovers. But she was leery of talking, of where it might lead. There was still a sense of unreality about what had happened with Clay; she preferred to keep things that way.

She stretched out the phone conversation as long as possible, but finally had to hang up, leaving her mother bemused but content. They would talk later to plan the small wedding that would be held in Silver Rapids.

Clay returned to the bed and sat on the edge of the mattress, running one finger down the length of Jennifer's arm. "Why *are* you negative about the whole thing?" he asked, surprised at himself because normally he didn't ask such direct questions. He suspected that Jennifer's feelings about her mother's marriage concerned him a great deal.

"My mother's a wonderful woman, but she's trusting to a fault, and she's always gravitated toward the kind of man who takes advantage of her," Jennifer said at last, surprising herself with her uncharacteristic bluntness. "Emotional vampires. They soaked up her unstinting affection and admiration until they'd strengthened their own egos, then moved on to more challenging game."

"Which of these . . . emotional vampires . . . was your father?" Clay asked carefully. He was in a rush, but what he was learning was central to understanding Jennifer. He had to take the time even if he ended up late for his meeting.

She shrugged. "Barry Allan was Mom's first husband, and I gather he was a Peter Pan trying to be Don Juan. I don't consider him my father. Biological coincidence doesn't count."

"So you're not close to him," Clay remarked.

"I've never met the man—or rather, the boy," Jennifer said without emotion. "He was twenty-two when he decided he didn't like being married and putting up with a six-month-old baby, so off he went to flit from flower to flower, not a care in the world. He's still doing it, from what I hear. Mom was just twenty-one when he left, but she managed to take care of me even though she was devastated. My grandparents told me what she went through; she didn't. She's never said a word against him, and after both her divorces she went back to using his name. She says it was less confusing socially if her name was the same as mine, but I wonder. Maybe you never really get over your first love."

"Did you?" Clay asked.

"I was determined not to follow the family pattern, so I made sure I didn't have a first love," Jennifer shot back with a forced grin. *Not until now*, she thought with another in the series of shocks she was experiencing this morning.

Clay had to struggle to suppress a quiet but simmering rage against the man who'd left deep, obvious wounds in both Jennifer and her mother. "How did your mom get along after she was left on her own with a six-month-old baby?"

"We went to live with her parents in Lansing and she got a job as a clerk in a department store. She's bright and capable, so she was doing pretty well by the time I was three. Then she met husband number two, and all of a sudden we were moving to—" She stopped abruptly and scowled at Clay. "Why am I telling you all this?"

"Because I'm asking," he answered, reaching for her and pulling her up into his arms. "And because you know I care."

"That's not a good enough reason," Jennifer muttered, unable to resist burrowing into the reassuring strength and heat of Clay's broad chest despite her deep-seated fear of becoming too comfortable there. "It's not right for me to talk about my mother's past to someone she hasn't even met. It's disloyal and unfair. Besides, I should be sending you on your way so you won't be late. I don't understand what you do to me, Clay. I don't know who I am when I'm with you. You were right last night. It's scary. All of it."

"I know," he murmured. He saw the clock ticking toward nine-thirty. "Dammit, we're finally talking and I really do have to leave." He'd planned to tell Jennifer all about Davey during a leisurely breakfast, and now there was no time. "My meeting should be over by noon, and since I have to head back to Detroit tomorrow I'd like to spend as much time with you as possible. How about lunch together? Someplace private—maybe a picnic."

Jennifer nodded. "I'd like that," she said quietly. "I have most of the morning to myself, so I'll shop for some food and fix something for us."

As Clay tightened his arms around Jennifer, he realized he had to tell her very soon that he was part of a package deal. He hadn't lost confidence that she'd accept Davey readily, but she might be justifiably upset that he'd kept her in the dark for so long about such an important aspect of his life. As he reluctantly released her and headed for the shower, Clay told himself he would simply make her understand that things had happened at their own speed, that he hadn't omitted such an important discussion on purpose.

And he hadn't.

Of course he hadn't.

At least, he hoped he hadn't.

Halfway through the meeting in a boardroom at Town Hall with George Foley and several local merchants, the mayor's secretary slipped quietly into the room and motioned to Clay, miming that there was a phone call for him.

Something was wrong, he thought with instant alarm. No one from his office was likely to pull him out of a meeting. Jennifer wouldn't do it either. Even if she'd had a change in plans, she would have left a message.

He was surprised when he picked up the receiver of the secretary's phone and heard Maureen's voice. "What is it, Mo?" he asked, puzzled but relieved, deciding she must have some information she thought he would need to know before his meeting ended.

"Clay, your housekeeper just called me," Maureen said without preamble. "Davey didn't show up at school this morning, and Mrs. Blair says he left the apartment at the usual time. She has no idea where he might have gone. I think you'd better get back here on the double."

Clay's fingers tightened around the receiver and he felt the blood drain from his face as a rush of horrifying possibilities hit him. "Thanks," he said through clenched teeth, battling a wave of panic. "I'm on my way."

"Something wrong, Mr. Parrish?" the secretary asked.

He was already starting out the door. "An emergency at home. Tell the mayor for me, would you? I'll be back in touch as soon as I know anything."

He raced down to his car and drove straight out of town, calling Jennifer on his cellular phone and leaving a message when he reached her answering machine.

Sick with dread, Clay had to force himself to think, to concentrate, where Davey might have gone. He couldn't let himself believe something had happened to the boy. If he allowed his worst fears to take hold, he wouldn't be able to think past the guilt he felt for not being there when his nephew needed him.

Kids played hooky, he told himself. They skipped classes and hung out at malls. They went to movies—though not usually in the morning.

If only Detroit weren't so big, Clay kept thinking. In a tiny place like Silver Rapids, it would be an easy matter to track down a boy who hadn't gone where he was supposed to go, but in Detroit . . .

In Detroit, he told himself firmly, he could track Davey down just as well. He simply had to use logic.

He began making calls as he sped along the highway: Neighbors, the owner of the comic-book shop Davey liked to browse in, parents of the few friends Davey had made in school, the school psychologist—anyone he could think of who might give him a lead.

Nothing.

By the time he reached the city, Clay didn't even go to his apartment. At some point in the discouraging telephone search and the constant seesaw between panic and reason, he had come up with an idea.

He drove to Davey's old neighborhood, a residential area designed for family living, the kind with big backyards and apple trees.

There was a park down the street from the house Davey had lived in. As Clay left his car and loped across the grass toward a grove of trees at the far end of the park, he found himself praying he'd made the right guess. If he hadn't, he didn't know where to start searching.

It took him a few minutes to find the tree he was looking for, and as he climbed the trunk using footholds designed for much smaller feet than his, the blood was pounding in his ears like a rhythmic, accusing chant.

He'd been this terrified only once before in his life, during the search for Davey's parents.

And that time his worst fears had come true.

Please, he begged silently. *Please, Davey. Be here.*

On Monday just before noon, Jennifer was in her Arts Council office struggling to proofread the galleys of a dinner-theater program, knowing she would have to do the job all over again later. Her mind wasn't functioning properly; she was tired from a weekend blitz of *Oklahoma!* rehearsals, and deeply perplexed about Clay.

All she knew was what she'd learned from the two messages on her answering machine, one on

Friday when she'd arrived back home from the market after picking up a few things for the picnic lunch, the second on Saturday when she'd been at a rehearsal. An emergency, Clay had said the first time. Everything was under control, he'd told her on the second call. He would explain as soon as he saw her again, "probably on Monday."

She was a bundle of nerves. Every creak and moan in the building made her jump, wondering if Clay had arrived.

She was worried sick about him. His voice had sounded so subdued she'd hardly recognized it, and she was certain the emergency, whatever it was, couldn't be about business. Clay didn't strike her as a man who would be that upset about anything but a very personal matter.

Trying again to scan the paragraph she'd just gone over twice without a single word or punctuation mark registering on her mind, Jennifer started at the sound of a car door slamming.

A strange expectancy gripped her, and when she got up and peered through the slats of the window blind, she wasn't surprised to see Clay's Buick parked on the opposite side of the street, Clay himself striding around the car and heading toward the Rogers building entrance.

Her pulse went into double time as she watched him, remembering the intimacies of a few nights before, seeing the strong male body under his gray slacks and light blue blazer as if she had X-ray vision. She still couldn't quite believe the things she'd done with him, the things she'd felt. Looking at him now, she was stunned at the realization of how familiar she was with all the ripples of muscle under his bronzed skin, the planes and hollows and textures of his perfectly sculpted form, the secret spots that could make him gasp with pleasure and groan with escalating need.

She went weak all over as she recalled that Clay knew her body equally well. It was unbelievable. How had she allowed such a thing to happen?

She still hadn't come to terms with the way he'd possessed her, not only physically but on every possible level. She wasn't sure she ever would.

As she heard the downstairs door and then Clay's footsteps on the stairs, she took a deep breath and tried to get control of her runaway pulse.

But she was about to back away from the window when one more casual glance toward his car brought her racing heartbeat to a skidding stop.

She stared through the open slat at the attractive young woman in the Buick's passenger seat and the little boy in the back directly behind her. They both rolled down their windows, the boy gazing rather forlornly after Clay.

Jennifer recoiled, suddenly trembling from head to toe. Good lord, had she fallen for a married man? Had she believed a male's glib lies after all the years of guarding against that kind of naïveté? Had Clay won her trust only to abuse it—along with that of another woman?

Giving her head a little shake, she turned toward the open doorway, waiting for him to appear, trying to sort out the confusing messages from her brain. Nothing was making any sense. Why would Clay take a chance on coming to see her when he had his family with him? What in heaven's name was he hoping to achieve . . . ?

"I'm so glad you're here," he said as he stepped

nto her office and saw Jennifer looking at the
oorway as if she'd been expecting him. He swal-
owed hard, thinking how good it was to see her
ven under the circumstances. He'd had a gut-
wrenching weekend, and Jennifer was like a burst
f sunshine with her tawny hair and peach skirt
nd the wildly tie-dyed T-shirt that was knotted
symmetrically on one side and held there with a
olorful parrot clip. "I just drove into town and I
was hoping I'd catch you," he added.

Jennifer stared mutely at him, trying to square
er mental image of Clay Parrish with the new
eality of him having a boy and woman who
were . . . what? Family? Had he come to explain
o her and brought the family along to allay his
wife's suspicions about where he'd been all one
ight last week when she'd tried to reach him at
is hotel? Was he zipping up to the Arts Council
ffice on the pretext of doing an errand so he could
sk his new mistress to be discreet?

"Are you angry?" Clay asked, taking a step toward her, then stopping without knowing why. "I
wish I could have explained why I had to leave
own so suddenly, but there were things I had to
ake care of. I didn't call you later because I wanted
o say what I had to say in person, not with a
nessage on your answering machine."

Jennifer lowered her hands to her sides and
urled them into tight fists, battling for self-
ontrol as she realized with utter horror that she
till wanted Clay, still felt the same intense and
rgent heaviness between her thighs, still longed
o melt into his arms and surrender to his kiss.
Ier response to him despite what he seemed to
ave done to her was the ultimate humiliation, the

final shattering of any illusions about her own
strength and integrity.

"What is it?" Clay asked, frowning. "I can't be
lieve you're annoyed that I had to cancel ou
picnic."

Either he was arrogant beyond belief or she wa
dead wrong about what was going on, Jennife
thought with a sudden flicker of hope. Had she
done it to him again? Had she jumped to the wors
conclusion about him on the flimsiest of evidence'
"So things turned out all right with your . .
your emergency?" she asked at last, sinking int
her chair before her legs gave out.

"Yes and no," Clay answered. He'd found Davey
but he still couldn't reach the boy. And the crisi
had made him realize how unfair he'd been in no
telling Jennifer everything right from the start
None of his reasons seemed valid any longer. The
were excuses. And now he had two situations tha
baffled him: What to do about Davey, and what t
do about Jennifer.

He took a deep breath and let it out on a slow
count, planning his words carefully. "There'
someone down in the car I want you to meet
Jennifer. Two someones, actually, but one i
particular . . . I should have told you . . . woul
have told you. That talk I kept wanting to have
planned to have on our picnic . . . I though
maybe we could have lunch, and you could see fo
yourself. . . ."

Jennifer's hopes faltered as she listened to Clay'
uncharacteristically clumsy phrases. Judging b
the trouble he was having with his explanation, i
was a difficult one. An awkward one. But wh
would he want her to *meet* his family?

Good grief, had she been living in a small town too long? Had she lost touch with how sophisticated people in cities were becoming?

Despite her panicky thoughts, Jennifer was determined to stay cool and controlled. "It's all right," she said. "I happened to look out when I heard your car door. You're not traveling alone this week. The lady is quite pretty, by the way."

"That's Maureen," Clay said.

Jennifer perked up. Hadn't she heard that name before?

"Mo decided to come with me this week," Clay went on, then paused and scowled. Jennifer didn't seem like herself at all. "There *is* something wrong. Will you please tell me . . ." Suddenly the truth hit him with a force that took his breath away. He couldn't believe it at first; then something inside him snapped. After all the agonizing he'd been doing the past few days and all the doubts he'd wrestled with, he couldn't deal with Jennifer's silent but unmistakable accusation.

"Nothing has changed, has it?" he said, his tone icy-hard and his eyes turning the color of cold pewter. "You've been ready to think the worst of me from the very beginning, and it seems as if nothing I've done or said, nothing I can ever do or say, will change that. I realize how the scene in my car must seem to you, and I'm sorry it didn't occur to me that you might look outside and see Maureen and Davey before I had a chance to talk to you, but I've had a few things on my mind besides trying to stay one step ahead of your instant condemnation. Maybe I can't blame you for being cynical, considering your experiences with men so far—starting with the father who wasn't a father. But I've had some disappointments myself, and they didn't stop me from trusting you."

No sooner were his words out than Clay wished he could call back every one of them. He'd overreacted. He was feeling guilty, so he was taking out his frustration on Jennifer. How could he be angry with her for thinking what she did? For that matter, he wasn't even certain what she *did* think! What had she done, except look stricken?

Passing a hand over his eyes, Clay suddenly felt very, very tired. What was he trying to prove? Wouldn't it simplify matters if Jennifer believed the worst of him? Wouldn't he be doing her a favor to let her keep on believing it? He had nothing to offer her but trouble. "One of us has been a damn fool from start to finish," he muttered at last, "and I have a feeling it wasn't you."

Jennifer opened her mouth to protest, but before she could make a sound Clay had turned on his heel and stalked away.

Eight

Clay was halfway down the stairs when Jennifer's temper flared.

She leapt out of her chair and started after him, but by the time she reached the front door it was closing behind him. "Talk about your dramatic exits!" she yelled as she yanked the door open. Its abused hinges let out an outraged howl, but Jennifer's well-trained voice was stronger. "I could take lessons on striding off stage from you, Clay Parrish!"

Clay was at his car reaching for the door handle on the driver's side when he realized with utter astonishment that Jennifer had followed him and didn't seem to give a damn about making a scene in public.

"Not that I expect you to bother filling me in on any details," she went on as she marched across the street, completely heedless of the traffic she was stopping or the passers-by who paused to watch the unfolding drama. "Go ahead! Walk out because I jumped to a perfectly logical conclusion based on the only evidence you've ever bothered to give me! I don't know the first thing about you! I didn't *ask* the first thing about you! I just went ahead and—" She stopped in the middle of the street and shut her mouth, suddenly aware of her audience—and of the two people in the Buick, both staring at her wide-eyed and fascinated.

She'd forgotten about them. Dear heaven, what if a little discretion *had* been necessary? She had no idea yet what the woman and Clay meant to each other, and the last thing she wanted to do was hurt the innocent parties in this mess.

Clay's fingers were still curled around the car door handle, but he hadn't moved a muscle for several seconds. Suddenly hearing a loud click, he realized that Maureen had pressed the automatic lock button. His window was shut tight, so even if he wanted to get into his car, he couldn't!

Jennifer was close enough to hear the same click; her jaw dropped as the pixyish woman grinned and winked at her, then spoke to the wide-eyed towhead in the back seat. "How do you like the show so far, Davey? Listen, buddy, if your uncle makes a move to come around to this side of the car, you roll up your window, fast. We don't want him to get in and drive off in a huff, do we?"

Uncle, Jennifer thought. Clay was the boy's uncle. But what was the big deal about having a nephew? And Maureen wasn't exactly acting like a jealous wife. What on earth was the man's problem?

"Good lord, what are we doing?" Clay said, striding back to Jennifer. "Are we the unofficial town fools? Are we staging a running French farce here or what?"

Jennifer rested her hands on her hips and thrust out her chin. "You tell me, Clay Parrish. You invited me for lunch and then walked out on me. Now, are you going to feed me or are you going to renege? Do you want to talk or would you rather stand here all day watching the cars line up?"

He wrapped his fingers around her arm and propelled her toward the Buick. "Maureen, unlock the car," he ordered as he reached for the handle of the back door. "And Davey, you don't have to roll up your window. Neither do you, Mo. We're taking the lady with us. All right?"

"Sounds like a good idea to me," Maureen said pleasantly, releasing the locks.

"I can't leave my office wide open," Jennifer snapped as Clay opened the door. "And my purse is up there."

"Get in," he said, unceremoniously thrusting her into the back seat as Davey skittered over to make room for her. "I'll go get your purse and lock up the office. Where's the key?"

"The middle drawer of my desk."

"Fine." Clay closed the door and turned to cross the street. He strode into the Rogers building, having trouble absorbing everything. He'd always been an intensely private person. Quiet. Controlled. Now all of a sudden he was providing free, boisterous entertainment for the citizens of Silver Rapids on a regular basis, and his co-star was a woman who kept him so off balance he wanted to throttle her almost as often as he wanted to make love to her.

He was elated that Jennifer cared enough for

him to kick up such a fuss, but throttling her seemed like the best idea at the moment, Clay thought as he bounded up the noisy stairs. He'd brought Davey along for the week to try to settle the boy down emotionally; this kind of foolishness wasn't getting things off to much of a start.

The purse and the key were easy to find. Getting Jennifer's office door locked was another matter. By the time he'd managed it, he was swearing quietly at the sloppy carpenters of forty years before, inept building inspectors of present times, and Jennifer most of all. Why did she keep insisting the place had to be protected? It was a mess. The redevelopment issue was simply another battleground that was in a state of cease-fire only because he hadn't unveiled any part of his plan yet. The woman was impossible. Infuriating. Why the hell had he gone and fallen in love with her?

He was heading back down the stairs when he realized he'd shoved Jennifer into the car with Davey and Mo without introducing anybody.

He muttered another stream of curses. Was there no end to his stupid thoughtlessness? He dreaded to think how much further into his shell Davey would be retreating by now.

"Here's your purse. The keys are in it," he said curtly as he climbed into the car and turned to give Jennifer the handbag. "Have you . . . are you all acquainted yet?"

"Yes, we are, thanks to Mo, " Jennifer answered, her chin lifted in defiance.

Clay raised one brow. Mo? A lot of formalities seemed to have been skipped over in a very short time. Women, he thought. They had their own communications system and it defied all understanding.

Glancing at Davey, Clay expected to see the hunched shoulders and distant expression that meant the boy was trying to make himself invisible. But the youngster was sitting up very straight on the edge of the seat, gazing at Jennifer, his eyes huge and—unbelievably—sparkling, his lips slightly curved instead of pressed together in the usual tight, straight line.

For the first time in a year, Davey seemed too enthralled to be depressed.

Lunch was spaghetti in a little Italian restaurant on Main Street with red-and-white checkered tablecloths, Chianti-bottle candles, and wax grape vines climbing over every pillar and post. The pasta was incomparable, and Clay figured the decor was so outdated it was probably back in style.

He was glad Jennifer and Maureen had established an instant rapport that kept the tension minimal. To his bemused disbelief, Jennifer actually gave Maureen pointers on how to deal with Sam Crane at *The Chronicle* and perhaps even get him to look at a Parrish and Associates press kit.

"You're helping instead of picketing me?" he teased.

"I'm not helping you, I'm helping Mo," Jennifer retorted. She stuck her tongue out at him, then sent Davey a conspiratorial wink.

Davey's tiny but quick grin amazed Clay. For the past year, getting any kind of a smile out of his grief-stricken nephew had seemed like an impossible challenge. Even Maureen rarely managed that feat, and she was terrific with the boy. What was Jennifer's secret? Perhaps it was the lack of pressure in her friendliness, Clay decided, sitting back quietly while the women chatted. Jennifer didn't make a fuss over Davey or put any pressure on him, but she let him know in little ways that she was aware of him and liked him.

Under Clay's pensive scrutiny and Davey's equally intent gaze, Jennifer felt slightly unsettled as well as curious. There was a haunting sadness in the youngster's depths that tugged at her heart, and the usual glint of laughter was missing from Clay's eyes. She couldn't help speculating about the circumstances that had led to Davey's living with Clay—a family tragedy seemed to be a foregone conclusion. And something had happened on the weekend to make both uncle and nephew extremely uneasy.

Jennifer tried to quell her impatience about not knowing even the most mundane details. She gathered that Maureen had decided to visit Silver Rapids this week as much to help look after Davey as to do some hands-on public relations work, including giving the mayor some tips about how to keep his foot out of his mouth. But why the youngster wasn't in school and what he did the rest of the time when Clay was away from Detroit added up to a confusing puzzle. What Jennifer found hardest to figure out was the relationship between Clay and his nephew. There was no question that Clay loved the boy; his affection was obvious, yet there was a deep-seated strain between the two of them. And above all, Jennifer wondered, why had Clay never mentioned Davey to her? Her chance to have some of her questions answered came when lunch was over, thanks to Maureen.

"Jenny, I think you and Clay have more than a few things to talk about, and Davey and I have plans of our own for the whole afternoon. For starters, your friend Neil is going to give us a tour of the television station. So if you two will just drop us off . . ."

"Neil's going to show you around?" Jennifer asked, astonished. "Neil Weston, the busy producer of *Showdown* and several other award-winning shows, playing tour guide?"

"Maureen and Neil have been getting chummy by phone," Clay drawled teasingly, though he was grateful to Maureen for arranging things so he could be alone with Jennifer.

"Neil's a pet," Maureen said. "And, I gather, single. I hope he looks as good as he sounds. Does he?"

Jennifer had to think about it. Then she nodded. "I guess he does. A lot of women find him very attractive and charming. I'm sure you'll enjoy his company."

As Clay paid the check, he was somewhat dazed by his lack of reaction to Jennifer's comments. While he prided himself on not having a jealous streak, Jennifer was more likely to arouse his possessiveness than any woman he'd ever known. Was he so cavalier because he suspected that Neil was helping Maureen play matchmaker? Or was it, he wondered with mild surprise, that he had an irrational sense of confidence that Jennifer belonged to him, so there was no reason to worry about rivals?

Given his suspicion that he ought to cut Jenny

loose for her own sake, Clay found the whole situation—and his own conflicting feelings—very bewildering.

"How much time do we have before you dash off to some rehearsal?" Clay asked Jennifer when they were alone in the car after dropping off Davey and Maureen at the station.

"Not much, I'm afraid. I have a junior drama class in less than half an hour. It's part of a special school program, so I can't cancel out or switch to another day. It's only a forty-minute session, so depending on your schedule, we could get together again afterward." She smiled and added lightly, "I'll even share my secret, spirit-soothing hideaway in the woods with you so we can chat without the whole town as an audience."

"That would be different," Clay answered with an air of preoccupation as he drove toward the small public park not far from the downtown area. "I have meetings tonight, but nothing for this afternoon."

Jennifer paused for only an instant before blurting out, "Why didn't you tell me about Davey?"

Clay bristled instinctively, but reminded himself that Jennifer had every right to ask the question. "Things happened between you and me all of a sudden. I know I should have told you about my nephew right away—"

"I'm not talking about whether or not you *should* have told me," Jennifer cut in. "I just can't figure out why you *didn't*. After all, we've known each other for a few weeks. Long before . . . before the other night . . . we were together on plenty of occasions when it would have been natural for you to mention that you were raising a child. Is Davey your so-called situation at home, by the way?"

Clay nodded. He needed to collect his thoughts before he could give her more details.

"I just don't get it," Jennifer persisted, frowning and shaking her head. "Why should a nephew who's living with you be such a deep, dark secret?"

Clay pulled into the park and stopped by the playground that was deserted except for a few preschoolers and accompanying adults. He remained silent. He didn't know precisely why he'd been treating Davey as a secret. He supposed he could blame the reactions of other women he'd dated. But blaming another woman was too easy. It was another way of trying to shirk responsibility that belonged only to him.

"This subject is really tough for you," Jennifer said gently. "Why, Clay?"

"A lot of reasons," he answered, resting his clasped hands on the steering wheel and staring off into space. "For one thing, it isn't easy for me to talk about the awful circumstances that brought Davey to me. The . . . the accident my brother and his wife . . ." He cleared his throat, then went on brusquely, "For another, Davey's a very troubled little boy who isn't pulling out of his grief, and I'm no father-knows-best. He ran away from home last week. That was the emergency that sent me racing back to Detroit. I was lucky enough to find him without much trouble, but I can't get him to tell me why he'd rather hole up in a treehouse in his old neighborhood then live with me. I can't get him to tell me anything, for that matter. I pulled him out of school for the week because Mo said she could use some time in Silver Rapids and offered to spell me. It seemed like a good idea to bring him along instead of leaving him in Detroit with the housekeeper and taking the chance he'd bolt again."

"Mo seems like a terrific person," Jennifer said, not really thinking about Maureen. She was seeing for the first time how emotional Clay was—and how deeply upset he was about Davey. She wished she didn't have to leave him for even a moment before they could talk properly. "I'm sorry I acted like such a dope back at my office," she said with a smile, deciding the best plan for the moment was to ease the tension.

"It was understandable," Clay murmured absently.

Jennifer gave him a mock punch on the arm. "You didn't act like a dope at all," she said in a bad imitation of his voice. "Anybody would have thought what you thought!"

Coming out of his reverie, Clay grinned and reached out to grab her hand. "Sorry, but you did act like a dope. That's okay; so did I. Do you think the whole town's buzzing about us?"

"Knowing the Silver Rapids grapevine, I'd say we'd had our fifteen minutes of notoriety by the time we were sitting down to lunch, which makes us old news by now."

"I hope so," Clay said, shaking his head in mock dismay.

They were quiet for a while, sitting together holding hands, both lost in thought again.

Jennifer didn't feel she knew much more than she had when they'd started talking.

Clay still found himself tongue-tied about the ultitude of questions that plagued him, and e couldn't say what was really on his mind. He ouldn't tell Jennifer he loved her. How was she upposed to react if he did? Fall into his arms and en accept whatever time and emotion he could are for her?

Jennifer looked at her watch. "I'd better get to e school, Clay. I preach punctuality to my kids, I have to set a good example."

Releasing her hand, Clay nodded and started the r. "What age group is this junior drama class?" e asked idly, deciding that anything more serious uld wait until later.

"Eight to eleven. Davey's age, basically."

"Maybe I ought to sit in on the session," Clay ked. "I might pick up some pointers. I could use me."

Jennifer smiled sympathetically. "You two do em to be walking on eggs with each other."

"Eggs that are already cracked," Clay admitted th a short, gruff laugh. "Sometimes I think avey's afraid of me, and the truth is, I'm scared of m. Scared of messing up, at any rate. And I seem be well on the way. I'm not like you. You were so atural with Davey, so pleasant and relaxed—I vy you your gift with children."

Biting down on her lower lip, Jennifer lapsed to thought for several moments. But when Clay lled up in front of the school, she suddenly niled. "Why don't you, Clay?"

He turned to look quizzically at her. "Why don't I hat?"

"Sit in on the class. Get some experience with her kids Davey's age."

Clay found the prospect hard to resist. He love watching Jennifer at work. And maybe he wou learn something. "Wouldn't the children be se conscious?"

"Not if you took part. I shouldn't have used t term *sit in*. There's no point watching passivel You'd have to roll up your sleeves and join the fun

"Jenny, I'm no actor."

She laughed and rolled her eyes. "No actor? T that to somebody who hasn't watched you make speech at Town Hall or win a crowd of hosti protesters over to your way of thinking. Anywa we're not at the *Hamlet* soliloquy stage in tl junior classes. We really just play games."

"What kind of games?"

"Activities designed to boost confidence, crea an atmosphere of mutual trust, stimulate imagin tion . . ."

"Exactly what would I have to do?" Clay aske amazed that he was even considering going alor with the idea.

Jennifer grinned mischievously. "You'd have be a kid again, Clay. Think you could handle it'

"I have my doubts. I'm not sure I was a kid tl first time around."

Jennifer made a mental note of the revealir comment. She wished she had time to dig for tl story behind it right now, but she didn't, so sl reached out and ruffled Clay's silky, wheat-color hair. "C'mon, Parrish. Go for it. Live dangerously

"Okay, you win," Clay said, shaking his head defeat as he opened his car door and loped arour to help Jennifer out. "It won't be the first time I behaved like a child in this town. Should I roll t my pant legs or what?"

Jennifer laughed. "That won't be necessary. Just
e yourself and don't talk down to the kids. You'll
e surprised at how quickly they accept you as
art of the group."

She hoped Clay would hang in for the whole
ass; she didn't want to leave him right now for
'en a little while. Besides, he obviously needed all
1e exposure to youngsters he could get. But
rivately, she figured he'd do well to last five
inutes.

Halfway through the class, Jennifer realized
1e'd overlooked a couple of details when she'd
ared Clay to become a child again. Most of the
ames she'd planned involved pairing off accord-
1g to size, and instead of being the group leader,
1e had to participate—as Clay's partner. She had
be a child right along with him.

It was an illuminating experience, Jennifer dis-
overed. The first exercise in a trusting your part-
er game was to stand facing away from him,
ands at her sides, eyes closed, feet together, then
ll straight back, letting go, counting on the
artner's catch. Jennifer had a hard time letting
, but she had to do it or lose credibility with her
ass, so she finally rocked backward and hoped
r the best. It took all her willpower to release
ontrol. Of course once she was safely in Clay's
rong arms, she didn't want to move away, but
1e paralyzing reluctance she'd felt at the moment
truth was quite a revelation. She couldn't help
ondering how she'd surrendered so completely to
m when they'd made love.

When it was Clay's turn to fall and hers to catch

him, Jennifer found that his trust quotient wa
even lower than hers. For a moment she though
he might throw in the towel and mutter som
excuse about having to go and condemn a buildin
somewhere. Then an eight-year-old named Vicki
piped up, "It's okay, Clay. Jenny's there, and she
real strong. But you gotta close both eyes tight. N
peeking."

Caught in the act of trying to cheat, Cla
laughed and finally fell back—rather halfheartedly
Jennifer thought as she used her whole body t
catch him, her breasts crushing against his bac
and her arms locking around his torso.

"Vickie was right," Clay said quietly when he'
straightened up and turned to smile at her. "You'r
real strong, Jenny." He gave her an intense
searching look. "And you were there. You didn't l
me fall."

"Perhaps you'd like to try that move again," sh
said with a feeble attempt at a teasing smile. "Thi
time without hedging your bets."

Clay slowly wagged his head from side to side
"One step at a time. I'm discovering that I don't d
much of anything without hedging my bets. I'
not sure I can."

"It's a good thing nobody grades performances i
this class," Jennifer remarked, beginning to thin
she and Clay had a lot more in common than me
the eye. "The two adults would fail miserably
Raising her voice so everyone could hear, sh
summoned the group to form a circle. "It's kids
choice time," she said once the youngsters ha
gathered.

"Jenny, can we play Laughing Lines?" one
them immediately asked. The other children too

up the chorus and Jennifer agreed. Laughing Lines was a fine idea, she thought. It was harmless fun, not likely to reveal startling truths. "Who would like to explain the game to Clay?"

Clay was surprised to see almost every child's hand go up and pump the air eagerly, only one boy seeming reluctant to be the chosen teacher. He reminded Clay of Davey, though this youngster's hesitant manner wasn't as pronounced as Davey's and his eyes reflected acute shyness, not infinite, heartbreaking melancholy.

To Clay's surprise, Jennifer zeroed in on the boy. "Brent, you don't look as if you're too eager to take the floor here, but since I happen to know you're a whiz at explaining things I'm going to ask you to do it anyway. What do you say you tell Clay what the game's about while all these one-armed bandits demonstrate it?"

Clay wasn't sure how Brent was reacting to Jennifer's gentle, but firm request, but he figured Davey would get physically ill under the same kind of pressure. It bothered him that Jennifer would push Brent when it was clear the boy wasn't ready to be the center of attention.

"Okay gang, places if you please," Jennifer said, clapping her hands twice as she strode across the circle to Brent and casually draped an arm around his shoulders.

The children scurried to form two lines.

"Take it away, Brent," Jennifer said cheerfully. "What are the stakes in this game?"

"People," Brent answered immediately, smiling up at her.

"Right you are. People. This is war, only instead

of shooting the enemy you win 'em over to your side. And how do you do that?"

Brent turned his shy smile on Clay. "By making faces and stuff. First one to laugh has to go over to the other team."

Clay grinned, beginning to relax a little. It seemed Jennifer knew what she was doing. She was handling most of the explanation while giving Brent the feeling he was doing it, and the boy was coming out of his shell without even realizing what was happening.

Coming out of his shell, Clay thought, staring blankly at Jennifer as an idea started forming in his mind.

He remembered noticing on her Arts Council schedule that she was taking registrations for summer sessions of her drama classes, and the answers to some immediate, practical concerns began unfolding in his mind.

No, he told himself. Definitely not. He'd made love to Jennifer without explaining to her what kind of situation she was getting involved in. He wasn't going to compound his selfishness by asking her to shoulder even part of his responsibility.

Not a chance.

No way.

Nine

"I can't believe this place," Clay said as he took a plaid car blanket from the trunk of the Buick and looked around at the idyllic setting that was tucked into a bend of Silver River just minutes from town. "How can a spot that's so easy to get to be so quiet and secluded?"

"One of the many joys of nonurban living," Jennifer answered with a smile. She picked out a tree-shaded, mossy rock overlooking the fast-moving stream. "How about putting the blanket right here?"

They each took a side and smoothed the length of plaid wool over the flattest part of the moss-covered rock, then settled comfortably onto it, Clay stretching out on his side and propping himself up on one elbow, Jennifer sitting cross-legged under the overhanging branches of a birch tree, her peach-colored skirt spread out around her.

She looked like a flamboyant tropical flower with its petals fully spread, Clay mused silently. No

wonder Davey had been so entranced. No wonder
Brent and the other children brightened at the
sight of her. And no wonder a jaded city planner
from Detroit felt renewed when he was with her.

He breathed in the fragrance of evergreen and
unpolluted air, listened to the splash of the rapids
and the whispery rustle of birch leaves overhead,
and felt the tensions of his body already beginning
to release. "You're right, Jenny. Your hideaway is
spirit-soothing. Is this section of the river the
inspiration for the town's name?"

Jennifer shook her head and absently picked a
clover blossom. "There's a far more impressive set
of rapids about half a mile downstream with a
park and picnic tables beside it," she said as she
began plucking the tiny mauve petals and sucking
the nectar out of them. "Even on a weekday it's
liable to be busy when the weather's so perfect. But
I've never seen anyone else come here."

Clay was trying not to be stirred by Jennifer's
unconscious sensuality. He didn't want reality to
be swept aside again by his unquenchable desire
for her. Not this time. "How did you find this little
nook?" he asked, using small talk to work his way
up to the important topics.

"I explore a lot," Jennifer answered between
nibbles on the juicy white ends of the honeyed
petals. "It's a habit I started young, when Mom and
I moved so often. I'd have spent my whole life being
lost if I hadn't made a point of orienting myself to
new surroundings. I did the same thing when I
lived in New York, so I got to know some great
out-of-the-way restaurants and shops, and even
some shady retreats generally overlooked by the
brown-bag lunch crowd."

"How long did you live in New York?"

"Almost five years. I'd majored in drama at college, and I honestly believed that I was destined to be the toast of Broadway. Truth moved in on me before very long and so did disillusionment. The more involved with the whole theatrical scene I became, the less I cared about conquering it. And I really started longing for small-town life."

"What was the last straw?" Clay asked, intrigued by the picture he was starting to patch together about her. "Was there one moment when you decided to walk away from professional theater?"

Jennifer smiled and leaned back against the peeling white trunk of the birch tree, stretching her long legs out in front of her. "I guess I forced myself to show up at one too many cattle calls for small parts in Off-Off-*Off*-Broadway plays. I was wandering around, a bad case of the blues and my latest don't-call-us under my belt, when I ran into an old college classmate who was working with a child psychologist using drama activities to help emotionally disturbed kids. I was curious enough to go with her to an acting class that actually was a sort of group therapy session, and all of a sudden I caught fire. For the first time I knew what I really wanted to do with all the training I'd had. I helped my friend with her classes and gradually realized that the same basic activities could be used with kids who weren't troubled in a clinical sense but still could use a boost. Then I took some night school courses. . . ."

"Night school?" Clay repeated, his voice strained as surges of desire tightened his insides and constricted his throat. Jennifer's satiny legs were so close, so inviting, he had to use all his willpower to keep from gliding his palms over their smooth curves. "To get a teaching degree?"

Suddenly aware of the sensual tension in Clay and feeling a familiar erotic languor spreading through her, Jennifer drew her knees up to her chin, tucking her skirt around her ankles. "I . . . I wanted to learn some specialized skills for working with children, that's all. I wasn't interested in being part of the formal education system. I don't think the kids would feel as free with me if I were a regular teacher. I'm just Jenny to them, not Miss Allan. I can lavish praise instead of giving tests and assigning grades. Schools tend to be places where children are judged constantly, and too often found lacking."

"Preparation for the real world," Clay couldn't help commenting. Jennifer's instinctive, physical withdrawal was ample evidence that she'd begun the process of emotional retreat. Now that she knew what the complications were, she was backing away from him, and he couldn't blame her. "Most of us are judged constantly, and too often found lacking," he added.

Jennifer wondered why Clay seemed rather bitter all of a sudden. "I'm no educational philosopher, but I know one thing," she said firmly. "Several months of unconditional acceptance have helped Brent a whole lot more than critical report cards did in preparing him to deal with the real world."

Clay fell silent, his thoughts returning to the idea that had crossed his mind during the drama class. No, he told himself again.

"What are you going to do with Davey once

school lets out for the summer?" Jennifer suddenly asked.

Clay started. Was she reading his mind? "The housekeeper will look after him, I suppose, though I'm not sure. My apartment is downtown, and there's not much wholesome stuff for a kid to do. But I don't think he could take summer camp. He barely copes with school. A year ago he was a straight-A student with a gang of friends and an outgoing personality; now his marks are plunging faster than a runaway elevator, and he lives in an unhappy little world all his own."

Jennifer spoke gently. "What happened a year ago, Clay?"

Clay took a deep breath and forced himself to utter the words that still tore him apart. "My brother and his wife—Davey's parents—were killed. A freak boating accident."

Instinctively, Jennifer reached out and took Clay's hand, lacing her fingers through his.

He stared at their clasped hands, then brought her fingers to his lips in a gesture so natural he was aware of it only after he'd done it. "I'm Davey's legal guardian. I never expected that clause in my brother's will to be put into effect. My folks aren't very healthy, so they can't look after Davey, and his maternal grandparents live in a little condo in a retirement community in Arizona. It's up to me to raise Davey, but I don't know what I'm doing. My life isn't set up for looking after a child. I love him, Jenny. I really love that boy. Unfortunately, love doesn't seem to be enough."

"It has to be enough," Jennifer said quietly. "But maybe you're going to have to change your life. Parents do it all the time. And maybe you're going to have to ask yourself whether you've honestly accepted that you *are* a parent now. You can't hedge your bets on this one, Clay. Davey will sense the slightest reluctance in you."

Clay's whole body tensed. "You're a hard hitter, Jennifer Allan. You don't pull your punches."

"Would you want me to?"

He shook his head slowly and smiled. "You wouldn't be you if you did. And there's a definite need for the Jennifer Allans of this world."

Jennifer returned his smile, but she was distracted, thinking fast. Did she dare suggest the obvious solution? She didn't want to appear to be using Davey to bind Clay closer to her, yet she was sure she could help him—and his beleaguered uncle, as well.

Finally she decided to go for it. A little boy was more important than her pride. "Won't you be spending most weekdays in Silver Rapids for a while?"

Clay nodded, staring at her again, wondering. . . . Impossible, he thought. It was too much to hope for.

"I run summer sessions," she said, forging ahead despite her dread that Clay would take her suggestion the wrong way. "Daily ones. Brent's enrolled, and so are quite a few of the other children you met today. . . ." She grinned. "And you've seen for yourself how supportive they are. What if you brought Davey here with you? The classes would keep him busy in the afternoons, and I know I could find him a wonderful sitter for the rest of the time when you can't be with him. I have an *Oklahoma!* cast full of potential candidates."

As she saw Clay bolting upright, looking more

interested than offended, she barreled on enthusiastically. "When I was looking for cottages for Mom, I ran across several that could be perfect for you and Davey—so much better than your hotel room. I don't mean to sound presumptuous, but . . ."

"Jenny," he said softly, taking both her hands in his. "It's perfect. You're perfect. I wanted to ask you about putting Davey into one of your classes but I didn't know whether I should. Are you sure it's all right?"

She frowned. "Why wouldn't it be?"

"What if he holds everyone back?"

"We don't conduct races, Clay. Davey will be fine, and the other children will gain empathy and leadership skills and all sorts of other wonderful qualities by helping the new boy along. You'll see. Trust me."

"I trust you," he said, his voice suddenly hoarse with emotion as he drew her into his arms. "I trust you enough to try to stop hedging my bets." He lowered his head to touch his lips to hers, intending the kiss to be gentle and completely undemanding; he wouldn't push her. What would be, would be.

But Jennifer's arms curled around his neck and her mouth met his with the eagerness that never failed to enflame him. She was like honey, hot and sweet, her lips parting and her tongue meeting his, the full length of her body molding itself against him. Wave after wave of passion washed over Clay, each more overwhelming than the last, carrying away all his built-up doubts like debris swept from the beach by a powerful tide. "Jenny," he murmured as he released her mouth to trail kisses over her arched throat. "What about you? Can you stop hedging your bets?"

"When we're like this I *can't* hedge them," she said breathlessly. "Clay, I want you so much, I can't think about anything else. I forget who I am. I forget all the caution that—" She stopped abruptly and sought his mouth again. "Make love to me," she whispered huskily, her lips brushing his. "Right here, right now, just love me, Clay."

"Oh yes, I'll love you," he said as he lowered her to the blanket. "Here. And now. And for as long as you want me to."

With Jennifer's eager cooperation, he rid her of her clothing quickly, as if jettisoning excess baggage—and allowed himself to believe, for a little while, that the emotional burdens that made her afraid of giving herself completely to love were as easily tossed aside.

When she was naked, and Clay stood up to shed his own clothes, he gazed down at her in wonder. She was an earth goddess from ancient mythology, he mused, her body strong and lithe and generous, her full mouth a constant reminder of her innate sensuality. Even her colors were the rich, ripe shades of nature—her hair fanned out to frame her face in an aureole of red-gold light; her skin was creamy and dappled with the sunlight streaming through the trees; her eyes mirrored the clear green of the birch leaves and glinted with the sapphire of the sky.

"I'll love you," he said quietly as he moved over her, parting her thighs and poising himself at the entrance to her infinite warmth. "I'll love you as much as you'll let me love you."

Jennifer's eyes glazed with tears as Clay held her

in his arms and filled her with himself. *As much as you'll let me love you*, she repeated silently, knowing he wasn't talking about physical love alone. She realized that she wanted all the love he had to give her, but didn't have the courage to accept it. She had to let go of all the defenses that had been part of her for as long as she could remember, and she wasn't sure she could do it. "Hold me," she whispered, clinging to him as if he could protect her from herself. "Don't let me think. Shut out the world for me, Clay. *Be* my world, for a little while."

Strangely humbled by Jennifer's almost desperate need to give him her trust, Clay showered kisses over her upturned face, the salty taste of her tears on his lips. "Let it happen, Jenny," he urged. "Look at me and know that right now you're all mine. I'm holding you and loving you and I won't let anything hurt you. All you have to do is trust me." He slid his hands under her body and lifted her for his deep, possessive thrusts, at the same time lowering his mouth to plunder hers, confident it was his for the taking.

At first Jennifer was aware of the cushiony, musk-scented moss under the blanket, the gurgling and whooshing of the river below, the chirping of a bird and the caress of a light breeze against her skin. Then she focused on Clay and gradually everything else slid away. She tasted only the mint of Clay's mouth and breathed in nothing but the multitextured fragrances of his body. Her hands stroked his sun-warmed back; her thighs tightened around his lean hips. His loving murmurs and rhythmic breathing were the only sounds she heard, and when she looked up, she lost herself in the fathomless gray velvet of his eyes.

She felt drugged, her consciousness altered by sensation. As Clay moved within her he stoked a fire that burned with unbearable intensity. Her voice seemed disembodied as she heard herself crying out Clay's name again and again, telling him what he was making her feel, begging him to give her release yet never to stop, and when release finally came she was overwhelmed by an exhilarating, liberating joy.

But inevitably, her old doubts forced their way back into her consciousness. If only they would *stay* away, Jennifer thought as she rested in Clay's arms. They were so deeply imbedded in her she wondered what it would take to root them out and be rid of them once and for all. They were a prison of her own making, and now that she'd experienced freedom she wasn't satisfied with any form of bondage.

Aware that Clay's evening meeting involved a press conference to update the media on the progress of the redevelopment plans, Jennifer suggested that Maureen should go with him. "I could take Davey to my *Oklahoma!* rehearsal tonight," she said as they drove back to town. "The show's on for next week, so we're in pretty good shape. I'll bet Davey would enjoy it, and it'd be a good way to start easing him into being part of my junior class in the summer."

"I don't know, Jenny. You'll have your hands full. Besides, it doesn't seem right for me to take advantage of your good nature."

Jennifer scowled and clasped her hands in her lap. After what they'd shared, Clay didn't feel free to let her keep an eye on his nephew for a couple of hours? "I'm not all that good-natured, and you wouldn't be taking advantage," she said with sudden coolness. "The kids are doing run-throughs with only a few stops and starts, so I'm merely an audience. I give them feedback after each act. But suit yourself; I have no reason to want to free Maureen up so she can help sway public opinion about knocking down buildings."

Clay reached over and curved his hand around her tightly entwined fingers. He was disappointed. Somehow he'd been optimistic enough to believe that Jennifer's hackles wouldn't be raised so easily now. Her emotional withdrawal was visible again in the sudden stiffness of her body, the lift of her chin. In a way, she was like Davey. Every time he thought he was getting truly close to either of them, he did something wrong and made them skitter away like crabs hiding behind the nearest rock.

"Look," he said firmly, "I don't know why you should seem hurt because I'm trying to be considerate. Would you prefer that I act as if I have every right to treat you like a baby-sitting service?"

"Yes," Jennifer muttered before she could stop herself.

Clay tipped back his head and laughed. "Okay, you've got yourself a deal. As long as you're sure Davey won't be in your way tonight, I'd be grateful if you'd help Parrish and Associates by freeing Maureen up for the press conference."

"Fine. Great," Jennifer said, rolling her eyes in mock disgust. "You're probably going to announce that the community hall won't be around long enough for the four-day run of our show, and I won't be there to picket you!"

Clay laughed again, but this time his amusement was a little forced. He wasn't going to make any such announcement—yet. The *Oklahoma!* run was safe, and his town plan was a long way from completion, but he had no intention of letting his personal feelings influence his decision about the community hall or the Rogers building or any other so-called landmark.

So many problems, he thought. Would he and Jennifer overcome them or be defeated by them? "What time does your rehearsal end?" he asked, deciding not to dwell on difficulties now. "Nine, as usual?"

Jennifer nodded absently, wondering why she was trying to help Clay with the press conference. Had he swung her over to his way of thinking about the buildings she'd vowed to protect, or had she surrendered to him so totally she no longer had independent opinions? Or was he simply right and she was preparing herself to admit it?

Dammit, she couldn't think anymore!

"Where will we meet if I'm not finished by nine?" Clay asked, breaking into her thoughts.

Jennifer considered the question for a moment, then said, "My place, I suppose. That way it won't matter if you're delayed."

Clay felt a pang of guilt about letting Jennifer take Davey for what could turn out to be most of the evening, but he said nothing; his guilt seemed to offend her.

They met Maureen and Davey at the hotel and the four of them had hamburgers at the Silver

Dollar Diner before moving on to their commitments.

Davey showed no emotion whatsoever about
going with Jennifer to her rehearsal—no enthusiasm, no rebellion, nothing. He'd be a tougher little
nut to crack than Brent, she realized.

When Clay dropped them off at the hall, Davey
obediently followed Jennifer inside. They were
alone in the building; Jennifer had made certain
they arrived early. "I hope you see a good rehearsal
tonight," she said cheerfully as they stood in the
middle of the large room. "You'll be the cast's first
audience, except for once when your uncle saw a
couple of songs. They'll be nervous."

Davey's forehead creased as he shot her a skeptical look. "Nervous? You mean of me?"

It was the most Jennifer had heard the youngster say at any one time. "Sure," she answered.
"They'll pretend not to be, of course. They'll probably even show off a bit, be boisterous, pretend
they're cool professionals. But they'll be wondering
whether you think they're any good."

"But I'm just a kid," Davey protested.

"Actually," Jennifer said, "I'm kind of hoping
you'll be my assistant tonight. I sure could use
one."

His expression turned wary. "I don't know how."

Jennifer laughed and shrugged. "Sure you do.
See those chairs by the back wall? You can start by
dragging a couple of them down here so we have
something to sit on. That'll give me a chance to go
over my notes."

After a moment's hesitation, Davey seemed to
decide he could handle that assignment. When

he'd set up the two chairs, the pianist strolled into the hall.

"Hi, Raymond," Jennifer called, glad he was the first arrival. She couldn't have planned it better Raymond Ackerman was the friendliest, most mature teenager she'd ever met. And to Raymond everyone was an individual, regardless of age or any other consideration. "Before you bury yourself at the keyboard, I'd like you to meet my new assistant," she said with a smile. "This is Davey Parrish. He's going to help me stay organized this evening."

"Yeah? That's good. Hi, Davey. I'm Raymond Raymond Ackerman." As Jennifer had expected Raymond reached out to shake Davey's hand. "You new in town?" he asked.

Davey's head wagged from side to side, then bobbed up and down, as if he couldn't decide whether being a visitor but not a resident qualified him as new in town.

"Davey is Clay Parrish's nephew," Jennifer explained.

"No kidding? Hey, Clay Parrish is the best thing that could happen to Silver Rapids," Raymond said, genuinely impressed, then grinned at Jennifer. "Right, Jenny?"

"Right, Raymond," she said, her smile becoming slightly forced. Whether Clay was the best or the worst thing that had happened to Silver Rapids remained to be seen. And whether Clay was the best or the worst thing than happened to her was an even trickier question.

The cast members started arriving, and Jennifer soon gave up on introducing Davey, though she made sure he met the teenagers who were most a ease with younger children. When it was time to start the run-through, she got him settled beside her and noticed that within moments he was caught up in the show. Since she'd told the boy he was to be her assistant, she decided to follow through and actually use him, writing suggestions on slips of paper and sending him to deliver them to the actors she pointed out as soon as they were offstage for a few minutes. Normally she simply gave notes at the end of each act, but her ploy for making Davey feel helpful turned out well. This time, the performers had a chance to incorporate her ideas and reminders as soon as they were onstage again instead of having to hold the thoughts for the next act or even the next rehearsal.

The run-through had a real zip to it, and Jennifer was pleased and proud of the way Davey visibly gained self-assurance as he got drawn into the action by the exuberance of the cast. It was almost as though the teenagers knew instinctively that the boy needed encouragement.

Laughing and feeling generally proud of themselves—they obviously knew they'd performed well, both on and off stage—the teenagers delighted Jennifer by including Davey in the good-nights as they left the hall.

Raymond, as usual, was the last to go. "Will you be helping Jennifer tomorrow, Davey?" he asked as he closed the piano lid and picked up his musical score.

Davey shrugged and looked questioningly at Jennifer.

"Would you like to help again?" she asked him.

"Yeah. It was neat," he answered with a shy smile.

Jennifer nodded. "Okay, I'll ask your uncle if it's all right. Because I sure would like to have you." She grinned. "And you saw for yourself how the cast liked the new way we did things. If I go back to the old style, they're liable to string me up."

Davey giggled.

A giggle, Jennifer thought as she turned away on the pretext of gathering up her things, her emotions threatening to get the best of her.

One small boy's giggle.

A standing ovation on Broadway couldn't even come close.

Ten

Clay not only gave his permission for his nephew to assist Jennifer at the week's remaining *Oklahoma!* rehearsals, he picked up on her technique of making the boy feel important and found ways Davey could help him as well.

The days whizzed by with little time for Clay to see Jennifer alone. He was worried, sensing that they needed their intimate moments. Jennifer's trust in him—and in herself—seemed so fragile. When she asked him to meet her at the Silver Dollar for coffee on Friday morning while Maureen took Davey swimming at the hotel pool, Clay was tense. She had sounded disturbingly serious when she'd called his hotel at seven-thirty to make the date.

He felt his stomach clench into a knot as Jennifer chewed on her lower lip, obviously having trouble saying what was on her mind.

"Out with it," he finally told her, unable to stand the suspense. Was she going to tell him she'd thought things over, and had decided there were too many complications to keeping the relationship going? If so, what would he do? Accept defeat graciously or fight to keep her?

Jennifer took a deep breath, deciding to be absolutely straightforward. "Clay, what are you planning to do about Davey between now and the beginning of the summer holidays?"

Clay stared at her. What was this all about?

She cleared her throat, then forged ahead. "Look, I don't mean to criticize Davey's school or your housekeeper or any of the arrangements you've made for him over the past year but I don't think he should go back there. You yourself have said his marks are dropping, so he isn't learning much anyway. Why not pull him out now and take a cottage right away? There are a couple of wonderful tutors here who can help him catch up on his schoolwork, and he'll be in a more wholesome environment. From the bit Davey's told me, all he does after school is go home to watch television and try to stay out of everyone's hair."

Reeling from the shock of what Jennifer was suggesting—especially when he'd been braced for something else entirely—Clay was having trouble sorting out his thoughts. "Stay out of everyone's hair? Did Davey use that expression?"

"Not in so many words, but how would you interpret what a little boy is really saying when he mentions that he has a TV in his room and keeps the volume low so it won't bother you or Mrs. Blair?"

"Good Lord," Clay said, suddenly hit by a long-buried memory that brought him back with a thud to the question of his nephew's feelings. "How could I be so blind, Jenny? How could I miss so many signs when Davey is so much like the boy I was?"

As Clay paused and lapsed into deep thought, Jennifer remained quiet, sensing that he had to sort things out in his own time.

Finally he went on softly. "My only brother was eleven when I was born. On top of being a little on the mature side to be starting a second family, both my parents had health problems, so I always felt . . ." He rubbed his eyes with his thumb and forefinger, then shook his head sadly. "I tried to keep out of their hair."

"Which is why you said you missed out on being a kid the first time around," Jennifer murmured.

Clay nodded. "You have a good memory. I wish I did. I've been spending the last year floundering about, wondering how I could understand a young boy when I'd never really been one myself. But I, of all people, should have understood what Davey's going through. What he thinks. All the crazy misconceptions and irrational guilts kids can come up with."

"As in both his parents being taken away from him, so he must have done something terrible," Jennifer said gently. "And then he found himself changing your whole way of life, worrying you . . ."

"Jenny, I swear I've tried not to give Davey the feeling he was a burden." And yet, he thought, there had been his own self-absorption. Even today, he'd been thinking about his relationship with Jennifer when she'd only been concerned about Davey. "But I suppose I did. . . ."

"You don't have to suppose anything," Jennifer

cut in with a frown. "You're wonderful with that boy. But for heaven's sake, you've had your own adjusting to do, your own grief to deal with. Give yourself a break, Clay. I've never known anyone to be so hard on himself. Now let's get back to basics. What do you think? About starting his summer early, I mean."

"I think it's great, but Maureen won't be here next week. . . ."

"We can work out the details," Jennifer said firmly. "Now, about the weekend. We're into the last big push to get the play ready, technical rehearsals, putting the final touches to the sets and costumes and props. . . ."

"We'll stay," Clay said, his sudden decisiveness more than equal to hers. He was beginning to see an important truth. An obvious truth. So obvious he wondered how he could have doubted it for a moment.

Jennifer blinked. "Both of you? I was going to ask you to leave Davey with me. He's doing so well, starting to relax with the kids in the cast—and on Sunday afternoon we're having younger brothers and sisters come to the rehearsal to get everyone used to playing to an audience. It would be a wonderful chance for Davey to get acquainted."

"I've already said we'd stay," Clay said again, shaking his head and smiling. He was so elated it was all he could do to speak calmly. "Davey and I will stick around for the weekend. I'll arrange to move into the cottage as soon as possible, and we'll both help get your show on the road. I'm a great set painter, remember? And I'll phone the school and my housekeeper this afternoon to tell them the new plans."

Jennifer was taken back. She'd expected to have an argument on her hands. She wasn't quite sure how to deal with Clay's unbridled enthusiasm. "What about your office?" she asked.

"Silver Rapids is my main professional project right now. I only went home weekends because of Davey. And there's no question in my mind that he's better off here."

"What about Mo? How will she get back to Detroit?"

"As it happens, your friend Neil has decided he wants to drive over to see a Tigers game this weekend. Mo's a baseball fan herself, so they'll have lots to talk about on the ride."

"But surely you didn't pack for more than a five-day stay," Jennifer said, unable to keep the consternation out of her voice. "What about clothes?"

"What about asking yourself why you're coming up with all these objections?" Clay asked teasingly.

Very good question, Jennifer thought. She had no answer.

"Trust me," Clay went on. "I think I can solve some of the practical considerations."

Jennifer scowled. "Well, I just . . . the thing is . . ."

"The thing is, Jenny, I'm scaring you. I wasn't supposed to cooperate so readily."

She bristled. "Don't be silly. Why should it scare me that you'd do exactly what I've suggested?"

"You tell me. I'm not analyzing; I'm merely observing. You've been scared since the day we met. Not scared enough, though. The frightened little girl inside you is losing ground to the strong woman who's prepared to take some big chances. Don't you see what's happening, sweetheart? You keep making commitments. Everything you do with me and with Davey is an act of love; it's a force you can't stifle. It's setting things in motion that'll change all our lives, and a few fears left over from your childhood won't stop it. I've been wondering how to conquer your resistance, but I just realized that all I have to do is sit back and let it happen. You're going to come to me, Jenny Allan. One of these days, you're going to drop all the pretense and every layer of protective armor, and you're going to come to me."

Jennifer downed what remained of her coffee in one gulp. If she'd been scared before Clay's little speech, she was practically catatonic now. If Clay was right, the entire existence she'd built for herself was under siege. She would be like her mother, giving her all for love. How could she have let such a thing happen? "I have to get back to the office," she muttered, getting to her feet.

"Why not?" Clay said pleasantly, then drained his cup and slid out of the booth before adding, "It's as good a place to hide as any."

"I happen to have work to do," she retorted.

"I'm sure you have. But you're still hiding."

"Stop saying that!"

Clay waited until they'd left the diner and were standing on Main Street, then he simply reached for Jennifer and hauled her into his arms. "In case I haven't mentioned it before now, Jenny, I love you. I don't want to pressure you, so I won't say it again until I hear it from you, sweetheart, but I do love you."

She stared at him, numb with shock and happiness and total panic. Finally, noticing that they were drawing a lot of interest from the morning shoppers, she managed a husky protest. "What kind of a place is this to say such a thing?"

"Considering the public nature of several of our previous encounters, it seems to me like the perfect place," he murmured, then cupped his hand behind her head and gave her a thorough, possessive kiss.

Jennifer was too startled to protest, and so embarrassed she couldn't think of anything dire enough to threaten him with. And, since she was melting in his arms the way she always did, she simply surrendered to the delicious sensations rippling through her and told herself she'd get revenge another time.

"Rehearsal tonight?" he asked when he released her.

Jennifer shook her head. "Friday's our free night."

"Then how about dinner and a movie? I notice there's a family-rated film on at the Strand."

Family-rated, Jennifer thought. Oh no. Jennifer Allan was single and independent. She liked esoteric foreign films. Family fare was for . . . well, families.

She remembered a valid objection. "I've heard the kids talking about that movie. They said it was boring." There, she told herself. She'd turned down the cozy outing. Then, to her horror, she heard herself going on. "I have a VCR. We could let Davey pick out a video he'd really like, and if you don't mind something simple like macaroni and cheese, I'll give you supper." She stared at Clay. Was he right about her? Was she incapable of resisting whatever power seemed to be directing her? And wasn't this loss of will exactly what made her wary of falling in love?

Clay crooked his finger under her chin and smiled down at her. "Davey and I will pick up a couple of videos and a bottle of wine. What time should we show up for what happens to be our favorite meal? And what goes better with macaroni and cheese—white or red?"

Giving in to what seemed to be the inevitable, Jennifer laughed and shook her head. "Six o'clock. Some modest but cheeky California rosé seems about right."

"Modest but cheeky. Got it." Clay planted a kiss on Jennifer's forehead, then released her and sauntered toward Town Hall, turning back once to wink and wave at her.

Jennifer watched him go, admiring the confident stride that made him look as if he owned the town and everyone in it.

Or at least one person in it.

The macaroni and cheese evening was the beginning of a hectic weekend.

To Jennifer's delight, Davey became a sort of mascot for the *Oklahoma!* cast and crew, who ran his little legs off with all sorts of chores and errands he seemed eager to do.

Clay, turning up at the community hall basement on Saturday afternoon to help put the finishing touches to the sets, was astonished and moved by the easy acceptance Davey had found with the teenagers.

On Sunday Clay joined a few other adults and a passel of youngsters for the show's first dress rehearsal. He half expected Davey to be frozen with shyness the way the boy usually was with strangers, but Jennifer and her extended brood didn't give him a chance to close down; amid much laughter during the intermission, they told him all about his uncle's adventures in junior drama class—especially how he had made such funny faces when they played Laughing Lines that everyone started giggling at once. For the rest of the afternoon, Clay kept catching Davey glancing at him as if the boy were checking to make sure he had the right uncle.

His gaze and his thoughts focused on Jennifer, Clay saw little of *Oklahoma!* Wearing a flowered skirt and a sunny yellow shell, her hair in a somewhat haphazard topknot, her smile proud as she watched her youthful performers, she was the most exquisitely beautiful woman he'd ever seen.

He wondered how he could find the patience to wait for her to confess that she loved and needed him as much as he loved and needed her. Since the only time he really felt sure of her was when she was in his arms, he ached to whisk her off somewhere and make love to her until her surrender was total and lasting. But there was never an opportunity.

On Monday, he and Davey moved into a cottage on a small lake about five miles from town, not far from the place Jennifer had reserved for her mother. Later in the day, Jennifer took them to meet a retired school principal who'd agreed to be Davey's tutor. Davey was a little shy, but soon warmed to Fred Burdine, a grandfatherly leprechaun of a man who claimed he knew a bright boy when he saw one, and young David Parrish was clearly one of the brightest. Davey beamed as though he'd been given a new puppy.

Clay smiled, understanding why Jennifer had chosen Fred. Obviously the man agreed with her image-building philosophy.

Oklahoma! was a resounding success; at the end of its first performance on Thursday night, Jennifer was inundated with enrollments for her summer and fall drama classes, and everywhere she went in town people kept humming and whistling the beloved Rodgers and Hammerstein tunes.

By the end of the following week, Clay knew he'd done the right thing in heeding Jennifer's advice. Davey had made more progress in the short time he'd been in Silver Rapids than he had in the entire past year. And at last there were precious moments of lovemaking with Jenny.

"You know, sweetheart," Clay said as he held her close after a stolen hour at his cottage on Friday morning while Davey was with Fred, "you really are a bossy little broad, but I don't mind because you're so often right."

She nipped at his shoulder. "What do you mean, I'm a bossy little broad?"

"Okay, you're not so little," Clay conceded with a grin.

Jennifer considered arguing, but decided she agreed with him on all counts. She wasn't so little, she was bossy, and if she did say so herself, she had a fair track record for being right. "Somebody had to take you in hand," she grumbled good-naturedly.

"Mmm. And I'm so glad that somebody was you." He rolled on top of her, resting his weight on his elbows as she wrapped her arms and legs around him. "So very, very glad," he murmured as they spun off again into their utopia of sensual bliss.

On the way back to town a while later, Clay chuckled wryly and shook his head. "Why do I feel as if we're having a clandestine affair?"

"Clandestine?" Jennifer said with a grin. "We haven't been exactly secretive." Still, she knew what Clay meant. She was beginning to feel the same way, wishing they had more time together, wanting to snuggle into bed with him and wake up in his arms instead of lying awake night after night, her body rebelling against the solitude. But she had to be practical, she reminded herself. She and Clay couldn't play house in such a small town with Davey on the scene. They were lucky to manage as much time together as they did.

She kept wondering precisely what Clay had meant by his remark in the diner. *All I have to do is sit back and let it happen,* he'd said, oh-so-confidently.

Let what happen? Her love for him? But they were making love already! Just what did he want from her? The words? But why should they matter, unless they symbolized much more?

One of these days you're going to drop every pretense, every layer of defensive armor, and you'll come to me.

Go to him how? Saying what? Offering what? Asking for what? The answers came to her easily enough, but Jennifer wasn't ready to face them. At least she'd progressed to the point where she didn't shut out the possibilities completely.

June was a month filled with small triumphs for Jennifer: Her bank balance grew every week thanks to the month's traditional rush of bridal

parties wanting special makeup; Davey w
changing from the walking wounded to a regul
kid right before her eyes; the summer arts festiv
was coming together beautifully; and the dinn
theater that was her brainchild had started ge
ting reservations from tourists all over the stat
thanks to several enthusiastic reviews from vis
ing critics.

But something was wrong.

Clay hadn't repeated that he loved her. He'd sa
he wouldn't until he heard it from her, and sl
understood. But she couldn't make herself say
couldn't take the plunge into the commitment sl
thought—but wasn't entirely certain—he wante
What if his love was an illusion? What if hers wa
She'd seen it happen so many times; people b
lieved fervently in their love, then it disappeared
even turned to disdain, and all hell broke loose.

On a Thursday evening late in the month, Cl
told her he had to go back to Detroit for a few da
They were walking in the park after grabbing
bite to eat at the Silver Dollar; Davey had wander
ahead, looking for weed specimens for an assig
ment Fred had given him.

Jennifer assumed Clay was starting to get cab
fever. After all, he'd grown up in the city, so the l
she found so blissful in Silver Rapids must see
terribly confining to him. That difference betwee
them was a serious warning sign, she told herse
"What about Davey?" she asked, taking refuge ir
matter that made her feel more sure of herse
"Does he have to go with you?"

"You tell me," Clay said, suppressing a grin.

"What's that supposed to mean?"

"Just that I can see the wheels turning. What's your suggestion?"

"Well, unless there's some reason for Davey to go, he could stay with me. I'm sure he wouldn't mind sleeping on my couch, and it would be a good idea to come here to the park with him on Saturday when there are lots of kids around, including several who'll be in his drama class. He's still a bit worried about facing that situation, so I'd like to ease him into it."

Clay didn't hesitate. "Terrific. I really appreciate this offer, Jenny."

"You have no objections, then?"

"Of course not. There's a lot I want to do in Detroit, and this way I'll have the freedom for it."

There was one thing about Clay Parrish, Jennifer thought. He certainly was frank. She pressed her lips together, refusing to give in to the urge to ask Clay what it was he was so eager to do in Detroit. After all, she told herself, it was none of her business. She'd offered to take care of Davey for the boy's sake.

Clay smiled as he saw the determined set to Jennifer's mouth, the familiar jutting of her chin. "Strictly business, Jenny," he said teasingly.

"Did I ask?" she shot back. "Did you hear me ask anything at all?"

"Loud and clear, sweetheart," Clay said, laughing. He was tempted to tell Jennifer what he intended to look into during the next few days, but it seemed premature to talk about something that was still just a possibility. A lot of things had to fall into place before he could make any final, drastic decisions.

He left on Friday afternoon, and Jennifer made a

point of keeping Davey too occupied playing card
to be uncomfortable about staying with her. Un
fortunately, umpteen games of rummy didn't kee
her from wondering how Clay was going to pas
the time in the city.

She and Davey had established an easy relation
ship by the time Clay got back to town late o
Tuesday afternoon, and she'd made sure the bo
had met several children his own age. It was n
surprise to her that Davey and Brent had becom
best buddies almost instantly, and it pleased Cla
immensely when he arrived at her apartment an
found the two boys engrossed in a board game.

Clay sent out for Chinese food, and after all fou
of them had laughed their way through
chopstick-wielding session and clumsily plucke
enough goodies right from the cartons to satis
their appetites, Davey and Brent challenged Jer
nifer and Clay to a few rounds of Pictionary—an
won fair and square. The boys had a rapport tha
was almost like mental telepathy, and Jennifer
heart swelled with joy as she saw Clay's obviou
delight.

Another evening of family fun, Jennif
thought, shocked by her deep contentment. Clay
mere presence added a special dimension to ever
thing; his spicy male scent pervaded her sense
his warmth and strength were magnetic, his v
brance electrified the very air. She found herse
wishing the night didn't have to end with Clay an
Davey going to their cottage without her. When th
moment finally arrived, she felt as if she couldn
bear it.

But she had to bear it, so she said a smilin
good-night and went to bed alone. Again.

The next day, she and Clay had lunch alone together at a little French-style bistro that had just opened. "How was Detroit?" she asked casually.

"Same as always," Clay answered. He tasted his vichysoisse, then nodded approvingly. "It's amazing how many great eating places there are in this town," he commented. "This one looks as if it's going to be another winner."

Apparently he didn't want to discuss his weekend—his long weekend, Jennifer thought. Fine. That was his privilege.

"Have I mentioned that I think you've worked miracles with Davey?" he said after a moment.

Jennifer couldn't help being pleased, but she gave a dismissive shrug. "Kids are my specialty, remember?"

"Kids and town planners," Clay murmured, his gray eyes caressing her. He'd expected to miss Jennifer; he hadn't been prepared to ache quite as much as he had.

She felt herself melting, as usual. All he had to do was look at her, she thought as her pulse throbbed wildly. What was she going to do when the summer ended and his town plan had been submitted? Clay and Davey would be gone, and her life would seem empty no matter how full her schedule was.

Unless she went with them.

Of course, Clay hadn't asked her. She was glad he hadn't. She was almost ecstatic. She didn't need another complication. Yes sir, she was thrilled he hadn't brought up the subject.

They settled into a busy but pleasant routine for the next three weeks, making love when they could steal a chance, enjoying the confidence they saw building in Davey, especially after several sessions in the junior drama class.

"I have to spend a few days in Detroit again," Clay told Jennifer toward the end of July as they sat under a weeping willow in the park, idly watching Davey play in a pick-up game of softball.

"I can keep Davey with me again," she said without hesitation.

Clay grinned. "I thought you'd never ask."

"Well, you know I don't want him to go back to Detroit until he has to; he's so happy here."

"I do know," Clay said quietly. He watched Davey field a ground ball and put the runner out at first base. "Good man!" he shouted. "Beautiful play!"

Davey looked over at his uncle, grinned, and waved.

"I should take him to Tiger Stadium sometime," Clay said as he waved back.

Tiger Stadium was in Detroit, Jennifer thought unhappily, but gave Clay her most dazzling smile. "Great idea. I'm sure he'd love it. How long will you be away this weekend? Until Tuesday again?"

"Is it okay if I call you and let you know? I might be a little longer."

"No problem," Jennifer said lightly.

Noticing a strained undercurrent in her voice and manner, Clay shot her a quizzical look. He wondered if he should tell her this time what he wanted to do in Detroit; his plans were almost definite by now.

But something made him hold back. Something told him that Jennifer wasn't quite ready to hear about what he was arranging. He only hoped she *would* be ready when the time came for him to make his final, virtually irreversible decision.

Jennifer and Davey were sitting on her living room couch playing hangman on Friday evening after Clay had left. There was an unexpected knock at the door, and Jennifer's immediate reaction was alarm. What if something had happened to Clay? The weekend traffic . . . "Mom!" she said as she threw open the door, overwhelmed by relief that a state patrolman wasn't standing there with terrible news. Instead, she was staring in shock at laughing green eyes and a smile so like her own it was almost spooky. Every time Jennifer saw her mother she felt as though she were glancing into some kind of back-to-the-future mirror and seeing herself twenty years hence—except that Laraine had decided to tame her wild hair by keeping it short. "What are you doing here?" Jennifer asked when puzzled surprise set in. "I thought you weren't coming until next week!"

Laraine Allan put her arms around Jennifer and hugged her. "I decided that you've been looking after too many of the wedding arrangements. I wanted to get here and help."

Jennifer laughed excitedly. "Where's your . . . Mr. Cross?"

"The name's Martin," a pleasant baritone said from the stairs. "Your mother couldn't wait while I parked the car, so I dropped her off first." As he reached Jennifer's apartment, he stuck out his hand and clasped hers in a firm, warm grip.

Jennifer's heart sank. Different, she thought. Her mother had said Martin was different. But he wasn't. He was the very type Laraine always had found irresistible—tall, lean, and good-looking. Jennifer didn't know what she'd expected, but a bit of flab would have been comforting, a receding hairline perhaps . . . anything to suggest that substance had won out over style this time, that character had counted for more than glamour. With his sky-blue eyes, silver hair, deep tan, and roguish grin, Martin was altogether too attractive to be anything but a rat.

Like Clay, a small voice inside her head nagged.

She blinked. Was that what she thought, deep down? For all the closeness she'd shared with Clay, did she still assume that his attractiveness automatically rendered him suspect? "It's wonderful to meet you at last . . . Martin," she managed to say politely, then stepped back. "Come in, both of you. I have company for the weekend, by the way." She turned and introduced Davey, who was looking decidedly uncomfortable about this invasion of strangers.

Laraine took Davey's presence in stride, accustomed to seeing children around Jennifer. Martin shared a man-to-man handshake with the boy, which softened Jennifer a little. Nevertheless she fussed nervously as she tried to get acquainted with her prospective stepfather, asking repeatedly whether he and her mother were sure they'd had dinner, whether they really insisted on staying at a hotel until they could move into their cottage, whether they were all set for their big day next week. With amused patience, they reassured her that everything was under control.

"My son and daughter-in-law will be coming in from Toledo," Martin said, then grinned at Davey

"They have twin boys about your age, Davey. I'm looking forward to seeing them; the last time we all got together was three months ago, and you youngsters have a way of sprouting up so fast a grandparent hardly knows you from one visit to the next."

Jennifer's eyes widened. Martin was a *grandparent*? They didn't make granddaddies like they used to, she mused. But she was beginning to feel better. Her mother was marrying someone's gramps. How bad could he be?

As the evening progressed, she found herself thinking that Martin wasn't bad at all. He'd been a widower for five years, owned a small chain of health food stores in Florida, and had a way of teasing and joking with her mother that revealed a solid bedrock of affection. He *was* different. The whole relationship was different.

Jennifer realized that she hadn't believed it possible for her mother to find the right man. She hadn't let herself believe there really was a right man for any woman.

When Martin suggested that he and Davey zip out to a store to buy some ice cream, the boy surprised Jennifer by going along without hesitation. She trusted the judgment of children. Martin had to be a good man.

"What a darling little boy," Laraine said when she and Jennifer were alone. "Is he in one of your classes?"

Jennifer nodded. "My junior drama group."

"He's so polite and quiet. Almost too much so. Does he have problems of some sort?"

Jennifer nodded. "Davey lost his folks a year ago."

"The poor little guy," Laraine said with genuine concern. "Does he live with foster parents?"

"He has an uncle . . ." The phone rang, and Jennifer pounced on it; Clay had said he'd call when he got in.

To her chagrin, she felt herself blushing furiously as soon as she heard his warm, gentle voice, and when she hung up a few minutes later, her mother smiled, her leaf-green eyes dancing. "Davey isn't simply another waif you're being nice to, Jenny. You're seeing his uncle."

Jennifer shrugged. "Sort of."

"Sort of? I'd say it looks pretty serious. And I can't believe it. I thought you were immune."

"Why should you think I'm immune?"

"Because I've never seen you this way. My sensible Jenny doesn't get all . . ." Laraine hesitated, obviously searching for the right word.

"Silly?" Jennifer put in helpfully.

"It's not silly," Laraine said. "It's refreshing. Tell me about this Clay of yours. What's he like?"

"He's a town planner from Detroit who'll be back there permanently as soon as he's mapped out a redevelopment project here in Silver Rapids."

"So? What have you got against Detroit?"

"It's where *he* lives, not where *I* live. I won't go chasing after him, Mother. Silver Rapids is my home. I simply can't . . ." Jennifer stopped. She didn't want to hurt her mother's feelings by saying she wouldn't spend her life moving from place to place, following this or that man the way she'd been forced to do as a child.

She didn't need to say it. Her mother knew. "I made some mistakes, Jennifer," Laraine said quietly. "I uprooted us when I shouldn't have—looking for love in all the wrong places, as they say. I'm sorry I put you through so much."

"You didn't put me through anything. It was what *you* went through that bothered me. I was always sure of your love for me, Mom, and nothing else really mattered. Even the rogues in your life were kind to me, so I never suffered a bit. But I hated to see you hurt."

"I know, honey. Do you know who taught me to stop trying to find my own worth in the approval of some man?"

Jenny swallowed hard, not sure she could speak past the lump in her throat. She and her mother were close, but they'd never talked with such honesty before. Never. "Martin?" she finally asked.

"No, baby, you did," Laraine said, with a tiny smile. "You taught me. I watched you grow into a woman who's more concerned with giving love than getting it. I watched you reach decisions that were right for you, and I watched you make sacrifices to build the life you wanted." She laughed softly and ruffled Jennifer's hair. "And I figured I must be one terrific lady to have raised someone like you. That was when I settled down to enjoy being me. By the time I met Martin I wasn't looking for anything, so naturally I found everything. And unless I miss my guess, you've done the same. I should have said all this to you a long time ago, Jenny: You don't have to be afraid of repeating my patterns. You're you, not me. If you're in love with this Clay, I'm willing to bet he's worthy of you." She laughed again. "As much as any mere male can be worthy of my paragon of a daughter."

Martin and Davey came back moments later to find the two women hugging and weeping on each other's shoulders. "Wouldn't you think they could save the sob stuff for the wedding?" Martin asked with a gruff laugh.

Davey put his hand on Jennifer's arm and looked up at her, his gray eyes wide with concern. "Are you okay, Jenny?"

She smiled, then couldn't resist the need to hunker down and hug him. "I'm getting there, sweetie."

"Me too," he said as his arms twined tightly around her neck.

"So what'll it be?" Martin said with a catch in his voice. "Pistachio, blueberry swirl, mocha fudge, or butterscotch crunch? We health nuts go a little wild on vacation."

The wedding was an emotional roller coaster for Jennifer. By the time the big day arrived, she was delightedly convinced that Laraine and Martin *would* live happily ever after—their every smile, every small act of kindness toward each other showed the depth of their love.

And the way Clay gazed at Jennifer during the vows almost inspired her to ask the justice of the peace if he was interested in a two-for-one deal.

But Laraine and Martin had promised to love and cherish each other for the rest of their days, and one stubborn part of Jennifer still told her that such a commitment was, for her at least, an invitation to failure and disappointment.

The day she'd begun to dread finally arrived in the middle of August. **PARRISH REDEVELOPMENT PLAN TO BE UNVEILED AT TOWN HALL PUBLIC MEETING** the *Chronicle* headline shouted in big, bold type.

Sam Crane's editorial suggested that Clay Parrish be given a fair hearing. Jennifer smiled as she read it; Maureen had done her work well. Of course, she'd given Silver Rapids special attention, managing to pay several visits to the town over the summer. Mo and Neil were a serious item.

Jennifer was delighted; she was fond of both of them. But she wondered: Were she and Clay still an item? Or was the plan-unveiling going to be their swan song? Clay had been working so feverishly to complete the project, she'd begun to think he couldn't wait to get it out of the way so he could head back to Detroit permanently. What little spare time he had was devoted to Davey as much as to her, and while she wouldn't have wanted it any other way she felt a bit lost. There just hadn't been much chance for her to be alone with Clay.

You'll come to me, she kept remembering as she stood beside Raymond Ackerman at the back of the crowded Town Hall and watched Clay take his place on the dais with Mayor Foley. Her senior drama class had gone on a bit, so she hadn't made it to the meeting in time to get a seat. *You'll drop every pretense and every layer of protective armor, and you'll come to me.*

Did he still want her?

Clay scanned the crowd to find Jennifer, smiled as he saw that she was wearing his favorite peach skirt and tie-dye top, then locked gazes with her for a long moment. Finally he made a few brief introductory remarks about the general philosophy that had guided his decisions.

The first phase of the project was the one that worried him. When Jennifer saw it, she was going to feel betrayed even though he'd made no bones about his opinion of several downtown buildings. He couldn't help shooting her a pleading look as he turned to the set of large flip charts on the easel beside him and turned the top one over. *Stay with me, Jenny*, he urged silently. *Don't get upset and walk out before you hear all of it.* At least she couldn't shut him out completely, he mused. Davey was at her apartment with her mother and Martin.

A ripple went through the room as he revealed the initial set of drawings, but whether it was shock or approval Clay had no idea. At this point he was concerned with only one person's response, and she was staring at him as if she'd never seen him before.

Clay hurried through his explanation of why so much of the downtown core had to be razed so a new and better Silver Rapids could emerge.

He turned to the chart for Phase Two. Maybe Jennifer would like this one better, Clay thought, wondering if he should have explained the whole plan to her privately so she would know he'd made provision for an affordable but comfortable arts council office, a decent gallery, and a theater-in-the-round, all to be housed in a refurbished Town Hall once a new civic center was built. Perhaps he was asking too much of Jennifer, wanting her to root for him simply because she loved him. And she did love him. Whether she admitted her feelings or not, he was sure Jenny loved him.

His confidence took a battering when he turned back to face the hall.

Jennifer was gone.

So was Raymond Ackerman, Clay noticed with puzzled curiosity.

It took all his professionalism to get through the rest of the presentation, and forty-five minutes later the standing ovation and hearty congratulations from everyone—including crusty old Sam Crane—meant nothing to him.

Jenny did feel betrayed, Clay thought sadly. So betrayed she'd left without hearing him out.

All of a sudden he'd had enough. He was through waiting for her to come to him. Striding along the hall, he made up his mind to go after Jennifer, tell her the vital bits of information she'd missed hearing, ask her to marry him, and quite possibly kidnap her if she refused. He knew he could get her to say yes eventually.

He marched through the open double doors with hordes of excited people spilling after him, then stopped dead, hardly believing his eyes.

Jennifer was standing at the foot of the Town Hall steps, looking defiantly up at him and waving a picket sign over her head. Raymond was behind her, along with Laraine, Martin, and Davey, all of them obviously prepared to give her moral support.

"Jenny Allan," Clay shouted, ready to strangle her for turning his own nephew and even his young ally Raymond against him over this town-planning foolishness, "are you *ever* going to give me a fair hearing? Do you know what you'd have found out if you'd stuck around for a while, the way everyone else did?"

"I don't care what I'd have found out," she yelled.

Clay impatiently raked his fingers through his hair. "Listen, you infuriating female, I've put my fancy Detroit condo up for sale! I've arranged to open an office here in Silver Rapids and make this town my base of operations, much to the joy of my public relations lady!" Satisfied to see Jennifer blanch and her green eyes widen with shock, he walked toward her and drove home his point.

"I wanted us to start hunting for a house with a banister and a place for a treehouse in the back-yard. I've made a very personal commitment to this town, and I've drawn up one hell of a good plan for its restoration, including building a new Town Hall and using this place as an arts center. Most of these fine citizens seem to like the idea a lot. And most of them seem ready to welcome me into their community. But do you have any idea why I've made such dramatic changes in my life? Do you have the faintest inkling of what would make a man turn himself inside out that way?"

"Read my sign, Parrish," Jennifer remarked stubbornly.

"Mr. Parrish," Raymond said quietly. "You really ought to pay attention to what's on Jennifer's sign. It's kind of important."

"You should, Uncle Clay," Davey put in, his eyes sparkling with inexplicable merriment. "You oughta see what Jenny's tryin' to tell you."

A burst of laughter from the crowd behind him made Clay scowl. He sighed heavily and tipped back his head to give in to the inevitable. He would read the damn sign, he decided. And *then* he would throw Jenny over his shoulder and carry her off to a cave somewhere.

His heart stopped.

Here I am, her sign said in hastily printed red letters. *Now what?*

He lowered his gaze to look into Jennifer's green eyes.

"Now read the other side," she said, twirling the sign.

Clay looked up again.

I love you, Clay Parrish. Will you marry me?

He stared at the words, then at Jennifer. "You wrote that before you knew . . . anything?"

"I wrote it when I knew everything that counted," she answered, then grinned. "But I admit that while Raymond and I were getting the sign together, I finally let him tell me what he'd researched about the way you work. About the sense of community you put into your town plans. The trees you make sure remain standing. The neighborhood feeling. I'm looking forward to seeing what the details are for Silver Rapids, but I love you no matter what they are. I wanted you to know I'd go with you to Detroit if you asked me to. I wanted you to know that I'm not hedging my bets anymore."

"But what made you leave when you did?" he asked, totally confused. "I thought you were furious."

Jennifer slowly wagged her head from side to side. "It was the way you looked at me when you flipped to that Phase One chart, Clay. I knew then how much I mattered to you. Actually, I think I've known for some time how much I matter to you. I just had to admit it to myself, that's all."

Mayor Foley suddenly appeared beside Clay. "You haven't answered the girl, Parrish. I don't know about Detroit, but around here, when a lady proposes, a fella doesn't keep her waiting. Are you going to marry her or not?"

Clay smiled. "Of course I'll marry her. I love her! Besides, what would the people of Silver Rapids do

for excitement if they couldn't watch us sort ou
our lives on every street corner in town?"

Jennifer turned and handed Raymond her sign
beamed a dazzling smile at Clay, and flew into his
arms.

Right on cue, Raymond stepped forward, raised
his hands conductor-style, and coaxed an approv
ing cheer from the crowd. The sound was deafen
ing.

By the time Clay raised his head after giving
Jennifer a long, hard, very thorough kiss, i
seemed to both of them that the whole town had
joined in the cheering.

Including, Jennifer realized as tears began
streaming down her cheeks, a happily smiling
Davey.

going to be a merry month, indeed, for all of us VESWEPT devotees with romances that are charm- delightful, moving, and hot!

irst, one of Deborah Smith's most romantic, dreamy e stories ever, CAMELOT, LOVESWEPT #468. Deb eeps you away to sultry Florida, a setting guaranteed nspire as much fantasizing in you as it does in heroine nes Hamilton. The story opens on a stormy night when nes has been thinking and dreaming about the love y recorded in the diary of a knight of Britain's Middle es. He seems almost real to her. When the horses on breeding farm need her help to shelter from the wind rain, Agnes forges out into the night—only to meet a n on horseback who seems for all the world like her ght of old. Who is the wickedly handsome John tholomew and dare she trust their instant attraction to h other? This is a LOVESWEPT to read slowly so you enjoy each delicious phrase of a beautiful, sensual, iting story.

Velcome a marvelous new talent to our fold, Virginia h, whose SECRET KEEPER, LOVESWEPT #469, is first published novel. Heroine Mallory Bennett is utiful, sexy—and looking her worst in mud-spattered is (sounds like real life, huh?), when hero Jake legher spots her in the lobby of his restaurant. From first he knows she's Trouble . . . and he senses a p mystery about her. Intrigued, he sets out to probe secrets and find the way to her heart. Don't miss this ving and thrilling love story by one of our New Faces 11!

oan Elliott Pickart is back with a funny, tender, sizzler, MORIES, LOVESWEPT #470. This is an irresistible y of a second chance at love for Minty Westerly and sm Talbert. Minty grew up happy and privileged;

Chism grew up troubled and the caretaker's son. E status and money couldn't come between them for th had all the optimism of the young in love. Then Chis broke Minty's heart, disappearing on the same night th were to elope. Now, back in town, no longer an ang young man, but still full of passion, Chism encounte Minty, a woman made cautious by his betrayal. Th reunion is explosive—full of pain and undimmed pa sion . . . and real love. You'll revel in the steps t marvelous couple takes along the path to true love!

That marvelous romantic Linda Cajio gives you her be in EARTH ANGEL, LOVESWEPT #471, next mon Heroine Catherine Wagner is a lady with a lot on h mind—rescuing her family business from a ruthless a greedy relative while pursuing the cause of her life. Wh she meets charismatic banker Miles Kitteridge she thir he must be too good to be true. His touch, his fleeti kisses leave her weak-kneed. But is he on to her gam And, if so, can she trust him? Miles knows he wants t passionate rebel in his arms forever . . . but captur her may be the toughest job of his life! A real winner fr Linda!

Welcome another one of our fabulous New Faces '91, Theresa Gladden, with her utterly charming del novel, ROMANCING SUSAN, LOVESWEPT #472. Fir devastatingly handsome Matt Martinelli steals Sus Wright's parking space—then he seems determined steal her heart! And Susan fears she's just going to be pushover for his knock-'em-dead grin and gypsy ey She resists his lures . . . but when he gains an ally her matchmaking great aunt, Susan's in trouble delightfully so. A love story of soft Southern nights a sweet romancing that you'll long remember!

Patt Bucheister strikes again with one of her best ev sensual charmers, HOT PURSUIT, LOVESWEPT #4 Rugged he-man Denver Sierra is every woman's dre and a man who will not take no for an answer. Lu Courtney Caine! But it takes her a while to realize just h lucky she is. Courtney has hidden in the peaceful sh ows cast by her performing family. Denver is determin o draw her out into the bright sunshine of life . . . and to melt her icy fears with the warmth of his affection and the fire of his desire. Bravo, Patt!

We trust that as always you'll find just the romances you want in all six of our LOVESWEPTs next month. Don't forget our new imprint, FANFARE, if you want more of the very best in women's popular fiction. On sale next month from FANFARE are three marvelous novels that we guarantee will keep you riveted. MORTAL SINS is a mesmerizing contemporary novel of family secrets, love, and unforgettable intrigue from a dynamic writing duo, Dianne Edouard and Sandra Ware. THE SCHEMERS by Lois Wolfe is a rich, thrilling historical novel set during the Civil War with the most unlikely—and marvelous— heroine and hero. She's a British aristocrat, he's a half-Apache army scout. Be sure also to put Joan Dial's sweeping historical FROM A FAR COUNTRY on your list of must-buy fiction. This enthralling novel will take you on a romantic journey between continents . . . and the hearts and souls of its unforgettable characters.

Ah, so much for you to look forward to in the merry month ahead.

Warm good wishes,

Carolyn Nichols

Carolyn Nichols
Editor
LOVESWEPT
Bantam Books
666 Fifth Avenue
New York, NY 10102-0023

60 Minutes to a Better, More Beautiful You!

Now it's easier than ever to awaken your sensuality, stay slim forever—even make yourself irresistible. With Bantam's bestselling subliminal audio tapes, you're only 60 minutes away from a better, more beautiful you!

__	45004-2	**Slim Forever**	$8.95
__	45035-2	**Stop Smoking Forever**	$8.95
__	45022-0	**Positively Change Your Life**	$8.95
__	45041-7	**Stress Free Forever**	$8.95
__	45106-5	**Get a Good Night's Sleep**	$7.95
__	45094-8	**Improve Your Concentration**	$7.95
__	45172-3	**Develop A Perfect Memory**	$8.95

NEW!
Handsome Book Covers Specially Designed To Fit Loveswept Books

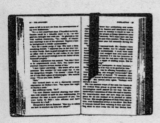

Our new French Calf Vinyl book covers come in a set of three great colors— royal blue, scarlet red and kachina green.

Each 7" × 9½" book cover has two deep vertical pockets, a handy sewn-in bookmark, and is soil and scratch resistant.

To order your set, use the form below.